Praise for
Me & Mom * vs. * the World
(Previously published as *Colonial Madness*)

"Making the most of a fun premise, Whittemore (*D Is for Drama*) adeptly fuses comic moments with a testy but loving mother-daughter relationship and intriguing details about 17th-century life."—*Publishers Weekly*

"Whittemore brings her customary insight and humor to every page of this funny and sometimes-suspenseful romp. The history goes down easy, with lots of laughs."—*Kirkus Reviews*

"The premise and plot are fun, the characters are identifiable, and the historical bits are well woven into the plot. Adventure-seeking readers wanting to dip their feet in historical fiction certainly won't be disappointed."—*School Library Journal*

Also by Jo Whittemore

Front Page Face-Off
Odd Girl In
D Is for Drama

Me & Mom
✳ vs. ✳
the World

(Previously published as *Colonial Madness*)

Jo Whittemore

ALADDIN M!X

New York London Toronto Sydney New Delhi

This book is a work of fiction. Any references to historical events, real people, or real places are used fictitiously. Other names, characters, places, and events are products of the author's imagination, and any resemblance to actual events or places or persons, living or dead, is entirely coincidental.

m!x

ALADDIN M!X

Simon & Schuster Children's Publishing Division
1230 Avenue of the Americas, New York, New York 10020
First Aladdin M!X edition February 2017
Text copyright © 2015 by Jo Whittemore
Previously published as *Colonial Madness*
Cover illustration copyright © 2017 by Monique Dong
Also available in an Aladdin hardcover edition titled *Colonial Madness*.
All rights reserved, including the right of reproduction in whole or in part in any form.
ALADDIN and related logo are registered trademarks of Simon & Schuster, Inc.
ALADDIN M!X and related logo are registered trademarks of Simon & Schuster, Inc.
For information about special discounts for bulk purchases,
please contact Simon & Schuster Special Sales
at 1-866-506-1949 or business@simonandschuster.com.
The Simon & Schuster Speakers Bureau can bring authors to your live event.
For more information or to book an event contact the Simon & Schuster Speakers
Bureau at 1-866-248-3049 or visit our website at www.simonspeakers.com.
Cover designed by Karina Granda
Interior designed by Laura Lyn DiSiena
The text of this book was set in Filosofia.
Manufactured in the United States of America 0117 OFF
2 4 6 8 10 9 7 5 3 1
Library of Congress Control Number 2016949504
ISBN 978-1-4814-0508-9 (*Colonial Madness* hc)
ISBN 978-1-4814-0509-6 (pbk)
ISBN 978-1-4814-8754-2 (eBook)

For my own crazy, quirky family.
I love you all to the moon and back!

Chapter One

No one ever buzzed the intercom at Mom's dress shop except Funk, the Fed Ex hunk, and that was only on Thursdays. Every week, he dropped off fabric, and every week Mom greeted him with an airy laugh and a smile traced in Hello Sailor lipstick.

So when the intercom buzzed on a *Monday* morning, Mom and I glanced at each other over the breakfast table. We were still in our flat above the shop, where I was scarfing down cereal while Mom splashed coffee in her mug of morning sugar.

"Is it already time to open?" She frowned. "Or did my sign for summer hours fall down again?"

"You still have thirty minutes," I said, checking my phone. "And your sign keeps falling because you used Bubble Yum to hold it up."

"Shouldn't you be going somewhere?" she asked, tapping me on the nose with her spoon.

"The museum," I said. "But not until ten."

"Good." She took a sip from her mug. "Then you can change out of those not-on-your-life jeans while I answer the door."

The intercom buzzed again, and she punched the speaker button. "Be right there!"

I glanced down. "What's wrong with my jeans?" One of Mom's designer friends had just given them to me for my thirteenth birthday.

"They're shredded, Tori." Mom slipped a robe on over her nightgown. "It looks like you threw them in the wash with a wolverine."

I pointed my spoon at her. "Hey, at least *I* do laundry."

"And *I* feed and shelter you," she said, opening the dishwasher. "I'll bet that's Sophia downstairs, wanting to see her new wedding dress plans."

Mom grabbed a manila folder from the plate rack.

"You *really* need to get that thing fixed," I said, nodding at the machine. "Or buy a new one."

"What are you talking about? It makes a great office utility *and* keeps my files lemony fresh." She pulled out a few sketches. "Besides, dishwashers are expensive."

"Since when have you ever worried about money?" I asked, placing my cereal box in the pantry so that it lined up with all the others. "And if you *are*, is buying new fabric every week *really* a good idea?"

Mom kissed my forehead. "That's not something you need to think about. I'll be right back," she said, waving her sketches.

"Pants, Mom!" I called after her. "People like it when you greet them wearing pants!"

"It's fine!" she shouted. "Sophia and I go way, way—"

Her voice stopped midsentence, followed by silence. After a couple of minutes, I poked my head out the door.

"Mom?"

I could hear her airy laugh, then the closing of the shop door. A moment later, she screeched and charged up the stairs.

"It was Funk! And he saw me in this!" She pointed at her robe. "And these!" She pointed at her pale, unpainted lips.

"Um . . . the natural look is in?" I suggested. "And you can't spell 'wardrobe' without 'robe'—"

"Ah, forget it," said Mom, fanning herself with a puffy square envelope. "This just means I have to answer the door in a ball gown next time."

I nodded. "Glad you didn't take it to a crazy place." I took the envelope from her. "What'd you get?"

"Not sure," she said. "Something from Massachusetts."

I opened it and slid out a folded letter and plastic DVD case with the words MURIEL ARCHIBALD'S LAST WILL & TESTAMENT on it.

"Who's Muriel Archibald?" I asked while Mom read the letter.

"Your dad's great-aunt who . . . apparently passed away last week," said Mom, wrinkling her forehead. "I'm surprised it took so long."

"Wow," I said. "So, obviously, you were close?"

Mom made a face. "Don't get smart. She was old and mean and disliked by everyone in the family. She hasn't even attended the last five reunions, so I just assumed . . . " Mom shrugged.

"Well, she was nice enough to leave you something in her will," I pointed out.

"We'll see about that." Mom slid the disc into her laptop. "Are you sure you don't remember her? You would've been eight last time you met."

A leathery-faced woman with sunken eyes appeared on-screen.

"Gah!" I took a step back. "I'd definitely remember *that* . . . I mean *her*."

Mom tilted her head to one side. "Believe it or not, she used to be beautiful."

"In the same way a hairless cat is beautiful?" I asked.

Great-Aunt Muriel shifted in her armchair, leaning toward the camera. A thick rope of pearls hung around her neck and swung heavily from side to side.

"Hello, nincompoops," said Great-Aunt Muriel in a deep, commanding voice. "If you're viewing this, then you've managed to outlive me. What a pity."

Mom and I glanced at one another.

"No doubt you're all celebrating and wondering how much money you'll receive," continued Great-Aunt Muriel. "The answer is: nothing. I've given the entire fortune to charity."

"Well, that's nice," I said. "Which—"

Mom shook her head. "Wait for it. . . ."

"Charity, my polo pony, was the only one who didn't bore me with the drama of her life."

Mom gestured at the screen. "There it is."

I looked at her. "She left all her money . . . to a horse."

"But Charity cannot appreciate the grounds of my estate nor its proper manor in the proper manner." Great-Aunt Muriel frowned and spoke to someone off camera. "That sentence was appallingly cute. Are there any more of these gems I should be aware of?"

Then, looking back at the camera, "Obviously, Charity has no need for the estate, so I'm forced to give it to one of you.

Since I loathe you all equally, it won't be easy to choose," she said. "Therefore, the recipient will be decided by a test—"

Mom paused the DVD. "Enough of *that*. You need to get changed, Tori."

"Wait, what's the test?" I demanded. "I'm great at tests!"

Most kids feared pop quizzes, but not me. I even had a special pen strictly for taking them. I used to have two, but my cousin Dylan stole one, hoping it would make him smarter through osmosis. Then he got expelled for hiding in the school's walk-in freezer and eating a week's worth of ice cream sandwiches. Now he lives in Texas.

I'd say his pen theory didn't work.

"Tori, I'm pretty sure this isn't going to be the kind of test you can study for," said Mom.

"We don't know that yet," I said. "That estate could be ours. Especially if I'm up against someone like Dylan the Dumbfounded."

"We don't need all that land *or* a manor," said Mom, walking toward my bedroom. "My business is here, not in Upper Snootyville."

"Well, even if we didn't live in the manor, we could sell it," I said, following her. "And use the money to buy a new dishwasher. Or make improvements to the shop. Like the fitting room."

"I told you we're *fine* with money." Mom opened my dresser, pawing through the neatly folded jeans until she found a pair she approved of. "And what's wrong with the fitting room?" she asked, handing them to me.

I laid the jeans on the bed and set to organizing my dresser drawer. "The lighting makes people look pasty, the mirrors make them look flabby, the carpet has tearstains from women who think they're pasty and flabby, *plus* the door doesn't close unless I'm there to hold it shut."

"You *did* say you wanted to be involved at the shop," Mom mused as she pushed the drawer closed.

I rolled my eyes and switched pants. "With inventory or window displays! And I'm glad you focused on the important part of that sentence." I opened my top drawer for a pair of socks and instead found a slip of paper. "'IOU some clean socks'?" I put down the note and looked at Mom. "Seriously? I had three pairs in here. When did you become a six-legged circus freak?"

She flashed me a sheepish grin. "Whoops! Sorry! I got chocolate syrup on one pair and had to use another pair to clean up milk I spilled. I was making chocolate milk, you see."

"I never would've guessed," I said. "Where's the third pair?"

Mom lifted one of her feet and pointed to it.

I squinted and leaned closer. "Did you draw faces—"

Mom quickly lowered her leg. "Hey! Why don't you go play the rest of the video and tell me what it says? If it's something easy, we'll do it."

"It may mean changing out of your robe," I told her. "Are you sure you can handle it?"

I returned to the kitchen, where Great-Aunt Muriel's image was scowling, as if she knew she'd been put on pause and didn't like it.

"Sorry," I told the image. "You were saying?"

I pressed the play button, and the video backtracked a beat.

". . . recipient will be decided by a test of wit and will. Archibald Manor was built during the colonial era, and I want the owner to appreciate it for all its majesty during simpler times. Therefore, interested parties will live in the same environment as our ancestors. This means no modern technology, such as electronics, automobiles, or grocery stores. Living purely off the land."

I shrugged. That didn't sound bad.

"For two weeks."

I grimaced. *That* sounded bad.

"In addition, you will face daily challenges to test your abilities," Great-Aunt Muriel continued. "The winner will be the person who has accrued the highest points and managed not to die from hunger or be eaten by other contestants." A phone number began flashing on the screen. "If interested, contact my lawyer—"

"A lawyer? You can turn that off now," said Mom from the doorway. "We're definitely not interested. And you have to finish getting ready."

"But—"

"Don't make me use my Bossy Mom voice," she warned. "You know how old it makes me feel."

"Fine," I huffed, getting up from the table and heading to my room.

Ten minutes later, my purse dangling off one shoulder, I peeked into the kitchen. Mom wasn't there, but her laptop was. The door leading down to the shop was ajar.

I sped-crept across the hall and pushed the disc eject button on Mom's laptop.

Nothing came out.

"BOO!" Mom popped up in front of me, and I yelped, stumbling back several feet. She took one look at my terrified expression and broke into a fit of laughter.

"What . . ." I glanced back at the shop door, which hadn't budged an inch. "Where did you . . . ?"

"In . . . the . . . pantry!" said Mom between giggles. She

pointed to our tiny cupboard, filled with food and just enough space to conceal one marginally insane mother. "I nearly suffocated, but it was worth it!"

"You know I hate being scared!" I huffed, and stomped downstairs.

"Have a nice day, darling!" she called after me.

I fumed and vowed revenge as my feet hit the sidewalk, but in all honesty, Mom was a pretty cool parent. Except when she was borrowing my socks, like today. Or once, when she packed me a sack lunch consisting of half a ham and two raw eggs. "I thought they were hard-boiled!" she'd said. "And your school said you needed protein."

She'd been raising me alone ever since my dad had died when I was a toddler. He'd been a navy pilot, and they'd met at the local base where Mom had worked altering uniforms.

Did I miss him? I think more than anything I missed the *idea* of him, of being a complete family. The reunions Mom spoke of only involved Dad's relatives. Mom had been on her own since she hit eighteen.

I stopped in front of a brownstone to wait for a girl with freckles across her nose and wavy brown hair like mine.

"You look troubled," she said by way of greeting. My cousin, Angel, flicked a braided strand of hair behind her shoulder.

The feathers tied to the end twisted on the breeze, and I was tempted to ask if she'd plucked them from a bird herself. Angel and her parents were survivalist hippie types.

"Did a package come to your house this morning?" I asked.

"With a message from beyond the grave?" she replied with a mystical waggling of fingers.

I smiled. "Yeah, Great-Aunt Muriel's video will. Are you and your parents competing for the estate?"

She nodded. "Living the way nature intended is what we're all about. If man and beast—"

I cleared my throat. "We're a block from your house now. You can drop the act."

"Thank God." Angel tugged the feathers out of her hair and crammed them in her pocket. When she pulled her hand back out, she was clutching a lipstick and dangly earrings.

"I don't know where my mom got those feathers, but there was bird poop on my windowsill this morning." She slid on the earrings. "My guess? The former owner was expressing some rage."

We paused for a moment so she could apply lipstick in the reflection of a car window.

"You know you don't have to go along with everything they want," I told her, pulling a stray feather from her hair. I tried to flick it away, but it stuck to my fingers no matter how hard I shook them.

"Honey hair spray," said Angel, blushing. "Dad thinks it's better for the environment."

Angel's dad, my uncle Deke, was a chemist. Her mom, my aunt Zoe, was an accountant. It's anyone's guess how they turned out to be ultrahippies.

"I know I don't have to humor them," said Angel, "but I'd rather hide the lipstick than get a lecture on chemicals. The last thing I need is another one of my dad's homemade butter-and-berry lip glosses."

"That actually sounds delicious," I said.

Angel curled her lip. "When it gets hot out it smells like my face is cooking. People call me Angel Food Face."

I fought back a smile. "Do you want some perfume?"

"Yes, please," she said, putting the lipstick back in her pocket.

I spritzed the air and she sashayed through it. I followed her, and we switched to a normal stride as we continued toward the museum.

"You're lucky we wear the same scent," I said. "And that your folks are clueless enough to believe you smell like that from walking beside me."

"Hey!" She punched my shoulder. "My parents aren't clueless. We're going to win the contest, you know."

"So, you really *are* going to compete?" I asked. "What would your parents do with a place like that if they won? Turn it into a butter-and-berry-lip-gloss factory?"

"Sell it," said Angel. "And use the money for a backpacking adventure across the U.S." She forced a smile. "We're all very excited to sleep in the dirt. Wheee."

I snorted. "If you're lucky, it'll rain and you can get a free mud bath. Most spas charge a ton for that!"

Angel wrinkled her nose. "What are you guys going to do if *you* win?" she asked. "Not that you stand a chance against us," she added with a wink.

"You don't have to worry about that. We're not competing."

"What?!" Angel stopped and turned to face me. "You have to. I can't rough it alone!"

"You don't need to convince *me*," I said. "My mom's the one saying no. She doesn't think we need the money."

Suddenly, Angel made a weird sound in her throat and stepped back.

"What?" I asked as she started walking again. I hurried to keep pace with her.

"Nothing," she said, coughing. "I just . . . ate a bee. It must have smelled my honey hair spray." She laughed nervously and swatted the air around her.

I gave her a look. "Angel."

She sighed. "Look, my mom is your mom's accountant, right? Well, according to her, Aunt Jill is in the red. Deeper red than this lipstick." She pointed at her mouth.

My heart dropped into my stomach.

Angel leaned closer. "Red is the bad—"

"I know it's the bad color!" I snapped. Mom had just finished telling me we were fine—*twice*. "Does my mom know?"

Angel gave me an exasperated look. "No, we're waiting to announce it at Christmas. Yes she knows!"

I shook my head. "How can we be losing money? I know she gets paid well. I've personally filed her invoices in the fork holder."

Angel gave me a weird look.

"I mean, yeah, she buys too much fabric in hopes that Funk will propose when he delivers it," I continued, "but—"

"It's not fabric expenses," Angel interrupted. "If I was eavesdropping correctly, Aunt Jill is paying a ton to have her shop where it is."

I glanced at the busy street around us and the people driving past in professional business attire. My mom sold couture dresses for special events. These weren't the people she catered to. But they *were* what made the shop's neighborhood so expensive.

"Then I'll have to talk to her tonight," I said, "and convince her to compete."

Angel raised an eyebrow and made another sound in her throat.

"If you don't stop that," I said, "I will find a bee and force-feed it to you. What now?"

"How much of the video did you watch?" she asked. "You only have until noon to confirm your entry."

I suddenly felt light-headed. "What?" I stopped and took a step toward home. But it wouldn't do any good to go back. Mom would still say no.

Taking a deep breath, I closed my eyes.

"Not sure if you're meditating," said Angel, "but at least move your arms so the pigeons don't come to roost."

"I'm not meditating. I'm remembering."

I reached into my purse and pulled out my cell phone.

"You're not calling your mom, are you?" Angel shifted from foot to foot. "Because she's going to find out I told, and—"

"No, I'm not calling my mom," I said, dialing. "I'm calling Great-Aunt Muriel's lawyer."

If Mom wasn't going to look out for our little family, it was up to me.

Chapter Two

"$\mathcal{H}$udson and Associates," a woman's bored voice drawled into the phone.

Since this was a serious, adult manner, I decided to handle it in a serious, adult voice. Which, for some reason, also happened to be British.

"'Ello, love, might I chat up Mister 'udson?" I heard myself say. "It's quite urgent."

Angel turned to me, wide-eyed, and opened her mouth. Scared of what she might say, I pushed her into a pile of garbage bags.

"Ow!" she shouted. "I think I fell on a pineapple!"

"You're calling for Mr. Hudson?" asked the receptionist. "May I ask who this is?"

"Victoria Grace Porter," I said in my most regal voice. "The . . . uh . . . First."

I could've sworn the woman snorted. "Thank you. Please hold."

Classical music assaulted my ear and Angel's fist assaulted my arm.

"Hey!" I dropped my phone and twisted away from her to retrieve it.

"Victoria the *First*?" she asked. "Planning more heirs to the throne are we?"

The classical music cut out, and the woman's voice returned.

"He's tied up at the moment. Can I ask what this is regarding . . . your Highness?"

I dropped the accent. "It's about Muriel Archibald's video will," I said. "I'm calling to tell him that we want to enter the contest. My mom and I."

There was a clacking of fingernails on a keyboard, and then the receptionist said, "You said your name was Victoria Porter? According to the late Mrs. Archibald's notes, you're the overly responsible child prodigy?"

I frowned. "How did you . . . how did *she* know?"

"Mrs. Archibald was in the business of knowing other people's business." I could hear the smile in the receptionist's voice.

"Meaning . . . ?"

"And so your parents are Hank and Jill," she said, evading my question. "The deceased hero and overly *ir*responsible seamstress. Correct?"

I bristled. "My parents are named Hank and Jill, yes. But that part about—"

"It appears your mother has already entered the contest."

I forgot to be offended. "She has? When did she enter us?"

"Herself, actually," said the receptionist. "She only entered herself."

I almost dropped the phone a second time. "*What?*"

Mom was competing without me? But we did *everything* together! We grocery shopped together. We took painting classes together. We went to the gym planning to work out but ended up reading magazines together.

"Why wouldn't she want me to come?" I asked in a small voice.

Angel gasped. "What?"

I shushed her with a wave of my hand.

"Doesn't say," said the receptionist. "Sorry, hon," she added with genuine sympathy. "My guess would be it has to do with your age."

"My *age*?" I repeated in a high, squeaky voice that didn't help. "That's the reason she needs me! She's old and falling apart."

"Your mother's thirty-four. I'm *forty*-four," said the receptionist flatly. "If *she*'s old, then I'm about to crumble to dust. We should probably wrap this up."

"I'm sorry," I said, heat surging to my cheeks. "Listen, my mom can't win on her own."

"Not if she's an irresponsible seamstress, no," said the receptionist.

I bit back a nasty comment. "Can you please ask Mr. Hudson to extend the entry deadline just until this afternoon when I can talk to my mom? We really need the money."

I crossed my fingers until the receptionist said, "Don't worry about it. I'll make sure you get a fair shot."

I hung up and clutched my phone to my chest. Angel squeezed my shoulder.

"You okay?" she asked.

I shook my head. "I don't get why my mom wouldn't want me there. Do you think it's because of school?"

"No," said Angel. "The contest is in a few weeks. That's what the lawyer said, anyway."

We both grew quiet until Angel snapped her fingers.

"She probably thinks you'll want to enjoy your summer and it'll feel too much *like* school," she said with a triumphant smile.

"You think?" My spirits lifted a little. "That's an easy enough fix. I mean, I'm going to the museum right now for fun, and that's as educational a place as it gets!"

"I'm positive that's it," said Angel. She tugged my arm. "Now come on. I want to go to the mall later."

We sped up our pace.

"Do you think I'm overly responsible?" I asked.

Angel laughed until it echoed off the buildings. "Not at *all*. Lots of girls carry a first-aid kit in their purse."

"Hey, accidents can happen anywhere," I said. "Although most usually happen within a two-foot radius of my mother."

"Well, I don't think there's anything wrong with being overly responsible . . . *if* you are," she added with a grin. "It's the perfect contrast to your mom."

I frowned, thinking of Great-Aunt Muriel's description of Mom: overly irresponsible. Part of the reason it bothered me so much was that it was right.

That afternoon, I sprinted home . . . or did my best attempt at it. After the museum, I'd convinced Angel to go to the library with me instead of the mall. My arms were weighed down with books on the colonial period so I could prove to Mom just what an asset it would be to have me along.

"Good luck!" Angel called when we parted ways at her place. "Text me later!"

When I burst through the shop door, gasping for air, Mom glanced up in alarm from a mannequin she was dressing.

"Tori!" She rushed over. "Is everything okay?"

I shook my head. "I . . . need . . ."

"What, darling?" Mom clasped my face between her hands. "Air? Water? For us to really exercise at the gym?"

I held up a hand to silence her. "I'm fine. I just need to talk to you."

Mom breathed a sigh of relief. "Give me a minute to finish what I'm doing. And let me take that." She reached for my stack of books, staggering under the weight. "Geez, are you an amateur bodybuilder?"

"No, don't—" I started to say as a copy of *Colonial Times* tumbled to the floor.

She sidestepped it and studied the cover.

"What's this about?" she asked.

"Weird, the librarian must have accidentally stacked it with my other stuff," I said. "So, how was *your* day? Anything interesting happen?"

"Not really." Mom shoved her hands into the back pockets of her slacks. "Just a couple of fittings. Boy, it's a crazy coincidence you'd accidentally be given this book today of all days!"

I shrugged. "What can I say? The librarian must be psychic. So—"

"Oh, come off it!" exclaimed Mom. "You're lying. You keep doing that head tilt you always do."

"And *you're* doing that thing where you put your hands in your back pockets!" I shot back.

"What are the colonial books *really* for?" asked Mom.

"Research! How come you don't want me entering the contest with you?" I volleyed.

Mom froze with a stunned expression on her face. "How do you know about that?" Then her astonishment changed to suspicion, and she crossed her arms. "How *do* you know about that?"

Whoops. Busted.

"Because . . . I'm good at deducing things," I said, keeping my head as still as possible. "Like Sherlock Holmes."

"Oh yeah? What did I have for lunch, Sherlock?"

I scrutinized her. "Nothing. There're no food stains on your shirt."

Mom frowned. "Go to your room."

"Was I wrong?" I asked as she pushed me up the stairs.

"Yes, you were. I ate a forkful of salad and half a cockroach." She opened our apartment door. "We're not ordering from Dominic's anymore."

"Gross." I wrinkled my nose.

Mom pointed down the hall. "Room. Now."

I stepped inside and said, "For the record, *you* lied too. *And* you left me out of a major life decision. *And* you hurt my feelings by deciding to compete without me." I let my lower lip pout to astronomical proportions.

Mom sighed and leaned against the doorframe. "Tori, I was going to tell you, okay? My decision to compete without you is for your own safety and sanity. You wouldn't survive a *day* of colonial life, let alone two weeks."

I flinched at the verbal sting. "And *you* think you could do better?"

Mom pressed her lips into a tight line. "Wait here."

She thundered down the stairs and returned a moment later with my stack of books.

"Here, pack mule," she said, holding them out to me. "Read these and write down all the colonial activities you come across and your *lengthy* experience dealing with them. We'll talk at dinner, and I'll decide your punishment then."

The instant the shop door closed, I stomped toward my bedroom as loudly as possible. My phone chimed with a text message, and I stopped to check it.

It was from Mom.

You're going to make an excellent ballerina. So light on your feet!

I stuck my tongue out at the phone and put it back in my pocket, walking normally the rest of the way. When I reached my room, I dropped the books, relishing the heavy thuds they made. Then I arranged them in alphabetical order, settling down with the first one.

"Salem witch trials, smallpox . . ." I paused. If Great-Aunt Muriel really *had* disliked us, we could be in trouble.

A lot of colonial life was spent farming and hunting and cleaning and weaving, from sunrise to sunset, and in the evenings people would read or play chess until the candles burned low. Then, the next day, they'd make more candles and do laundry and other household chores.

I jotted down a list of colonial activities on one half of a sheet of paper and Mom's and my experience levels on the other.

The results did *not* look good. For either of us.

Where farming was concerned, I'd once grown a lima bean in a Styrofoam cup for a science project, but we wouldn't have access to Styrofoam, and lima beans were nasty anyway. Mom had some mushroom-looking things sprouting in her closet, but I was pretty sure that was by accident.

Hunting? Neither of us had hunted for anything but bargains at the mall. Although Mom could be ferocious if an argyle sweater was up for grabs. All we needed to find were some fashionably dressed deer.

I already did the household chores, so that wouldn't be *too* bad, except I'd be doing the laundry by hand and, according to my research, I'd have to make my own soap from animal fat.

In the middle of all the reading, exhaustion caught up with me and I dozed off. I woke with a blanket thrown over me and the scent of Chinese takeout luring from the kitchen. Wrapping the blanket around my shoulders, I padded down the hall to see Mom scooping food from takeout boxes onto plates.

"I see you got a lot of research done," she said with a wry smile. "You'll be happy to hear that the blanket you're wearing *isn't* riddled with smallpox."

"How do you know about that?" I asked, sitting at the table.

It was something *I'd* just learned in the colonial books, how settlers gave Native Americans "peace offerings" of blankets covered in smallpox.

Mom handed my plate over. "I know many things. Do you have your list?"

I held it up for her inspection while she ate an egg roll. Her eyes scanned the page and crinkled with amusement.

"Tori, if all this was true and we were as incompetent as you think," she said, "we wouldn't stand a chance."

I turned the list so I could read it. "Am I missing something?"

Mom nodded and pointed at the paper, smearing grease on it. "I can do everything on that list except carpentry."

I shot her a withering look and wiped the page clean. "Yeah, right. You're *that* old."

She smirked. "No, but I *did* spend two summers in college working at a wilderness camp, and when I was your age I helped on my grandpa's farm."

My mouth dropped open. "You? Doing manual labor?"

"How do you think I got started making dresses?" she said with a smile. "You shouldn't underestimate your mama, little girl. If it came down to it, I could even weave us some blankets."

I pushed my food around on my plate. "Will it come down to that?"

Mom stopped with a fork raised to her mouth. "Huh?"

"Angel told me we have money problems," I explained. "And that's why I was calling Mr. Hudson. To enter us in the contest."

Mom put down the fork and reached over to stroke my hair. "That's *my* concern, not yours."

"No, it affects me, so it's *my* concern too," I said, pulling away from her. "Especially if I can help you win."

Mom sighed.

"You know I'm supersmart, so I learn quickly," I continued. "And I don't eat much and I don't take up much space and I won't get in the way, and Angel's parents are letting *her* go." I batted my eyelashes. "And you love me, right?"

"Of course I do," said Mom. "But—"

"It'll be like camping for two weeks!" I said. "And you know we won't be in any real danger."

"Well, that's true, but—"

"And we'd have *sooo* much fun together," I said.

Mom paused and smiled. "We really would."

I smiled hopefully back. "So . . . I'm in?"

Instead of answering, Mom speared a piece of sesame chicken and chewed it thoughtfully. I didn't want to pressure her *out* of the decision, so I started eating too.

She finished all her chicken and the other half of her egg roll before she finally leaned forward and said, "You can compete with me on one condition."

I sat up straighter in my chair and assumed a serious expression.

"Promise me," said Mom, "that you won't worry about money anymore. That you'll enjoy the experience . . . even if we don't win."

"Oh, we'll win," I told her.

Mom raised an eyebrow at me.

"But I promise."

"Okay." Mom nodded. "Let's call Hudson and Associates and tell them we need *two* tickets to Boston."

I grinned and held up my phone. "Already have them on speed dial."

Chapter Three

A few weeks later, Mom and I were trudging through airport security behind a group of businessmen. I watched them hoist briefcases and duffel bags onto the X-ray conveyor belt. Then I watched Mom carrying the one backpack *we'd* brought.

"We should've packed more than magazines and bananas," I told her. "We look suspicious."

"Of what? Being monkeys in disguise?" Mom dropped the backpack and her shoes on the X-ray conveyor belt.

"We could've at least brought spare underwear," I whispered, placing my shoes next to hers. "What if our plane crashes and we're stranded?"

Mom blinked at me. "Unless your spare underwear has a map in it, I don't think it would be very helpful."

The security guard gave us a strange look but signaled Mom to step through the metal detector.

"Besides," she said, "you know the rules of the competition. Everything that isn't medically necessary is going to be taken from us when we get there. Why weigh ourselves down with extra bags to keep track of?"

"You never plan for emergencies," I told her, passing through the metal detector. "That's your problem."

"And you worry too much," said Mom. "That's your problem."

She collected our belongings off the conveyor belt and pointed at a burger joint inside the terminal. "Let's have one last filling meal before we're forced to eat squirrel-on-a-stick."

"Okay," I said. "But hurry, so Angel and Aunt Zoe and Uncle Deke don't see."

Mom made a face. "Good call. I don't want to hear about their run-in with the crying cow again."

"Like it could even *read* the Burger King bag," I added, slipping my shoes back on.

We wolfed down our food in record time and were browsing a candy store when my cousin and her parents joined us.

"Hey!" Angel and I greeted each other with big grins.

Aunt Zoe hugged me and then Mom. When she pulled away, her nostrils quivered.

"You've been eating beef." Aunt Zoe reached into the pocket of her yoga jacket and pulled out a protein bar. "Nobody died to make *my* lunch."

"Don't sta-art," Uncle Deke singsonged under his breath, leaning over to hug me.

"This is new." I poked at his beard. "Are you carrying extra supplies in there?"

"My dad's packing all kinds of crumbs from breakfast," said Angel, smiling at him. "There's a whole piece of toast nestled in there."

"Are you sure it's not in . . . here?" He grabbed Angel and tickled her armpit until she doubled over with laughter.

I always liked watching Angel and Uncle Deke playing together. Sometimes I wondered if my dad and I would have been like that. My mom says I take after him a lot, so we probably would have spent most of our time trading sarcastic barbs and learning at museums together. When Mom and I go to museums, she cracks jokes the whole way, but I just want to study fossils in peace.

"Save your energy, you two," Aunt Zoe told Angel and Uncle Deke. "We don't know how much vegan protein we'll find during the contest."

Mom raised an eyebrow. "Really? You're staying vegan during this? I'm pretty sure the Pilgrims didn't have Tofurkey at the first Thanksgiving."

Aunt Zoe took a bite of her protein bar. "There are other legumes."

"Not to mention milk made from said legumes," added Uncle Deke.

My interest in legumes was down to le nothing, so I turned to Angel while our parents talked. The eagerness on her face had vanished, and she yawned wide enough for me to see a poppy seed stuck in her molar.

"You just woke up a few hours ago! How are you already tired?" I asked. "It can't be from all the toothbrushing you did."

"Huh?" Angel ran her tongue over her teeth. "No, we stayed up until one this morning planning our strategy."

"Strategy?" I repeated.

"Yeah. Didn't *you* guys?"

I scoffed. "We did one better. We actually practiced cooking over a fire."

We actually roasted marshmallows over the stove.

"Why didn't you just let your parents talk while you slept?" I asked.

Not that I'd followed my own advice. While Mom went into a sugar coma, I'd stayed up reading about edible plants.

Sometimes, I wish I could actually be the kid in our crazy dynamic.

Angel shook her head and yawned again. "My folks were really happy that I'm so . . . excited."

I regarded her dull eyes and blank expression. "This is you excited? I've seen couches show more emotion."

She stuck out her tongue. "I'm fake excited. It makes them happy."

"That seems healthy," I said. "Also, you have aluminum foil in your hair."

"It's from breakfast," she said, feeling around for it. I plucked it loose and handed it to her.

"Perfect for a fishing lure," she said. "Fish think shiny things are minnows."

"Too bad it's not from colonial times," I said, squishing it between my fingers.

"Again, it doesn't have to be foil. It just has to be shiny. Clearly you have much to learn about survival," said Angel. "You don't take advantage of your surroundings."

"Sure I do," I said as we followed our parents to the gate. "Watch as I take advantage of my mother."

I hurried to catch Mom and tugged at her sleeve. "Can I have change for the penny squasher, please?"

I loved the souvenir machines that would flatten a penny and print an image on it. It was kind of an obsession of mine that started as an obsession of my dad's. My mom said he always had pockets of loose change, and any time he was somewhere that had one of those machines, he'd get a flattened penny in every pattern. There weren't many ways for me to bond with a dead man, but it was better than Mom's idea of holding a séance.

Uncle Deke reached into his pocket and fished out a handful of coins. "Here." He offered them to me. "I'll be three pounds lighter if you take them."

Mom smirked. "Looks like you picked up someone's bad habit."

"Actually," said Uncle Deke with a grin, "he picked it up from me."

The adults stood around and watched Angel and me flatten pennies until it was time to board our flight. When the plane touched down in Boston, Dylan and his dad, my Uncle Max, were waiting for us at the gate.

"Hey, future runners-up!" Uncle Max greeted us with a tip of his cowboy hat. After he and Dylan moved away, he'd become a cattle baron out in Texas and was now probably the richest living member of our family.

Uncle Max shook hands with Uncle Deke and kissed Mom and Aunt Zoe on the cheek. Then he turned to Dylan. "Say hi, son!"

"Hey, future losers," mumbled Dylan, not bothering to look up from the frozen yogurt he was eating.

For a kid who came from money, Dylan dressed like he came from a Dumpster. His cargo shorts were baggy and frayed, his T-shirt was stained, and his hair was a shaggy nightmare.

"That's a healthy snack," Aunt Zoe told him with an encouraging smile. "All that active bacteria is good for you."

Dylan stopped midbite and scowled at her. "Gross." He spit the yogurt back in his cup and turned to Uncle Max. "Give me money for ice cream."

"Now, Dylan, you know that's a bad idea." Uncle Max chuckled again and turned to us, tapping his head. "He gets brain freeze."

"Hard to imagine," I said. Mom nudged me.

"Whatever," said Dylan. "I'm gonna go talk to people that matter." He pulled a phone from his pocket and wandered off.

Uncle Max shrugged at us apologetically. "Since his mother and I divorced, he's been going through a rough stage. At least, that's what the therapist says."

I had a feeling the therapist said more than that . . . like "Get out!" or "I can't help" or "Have you thought of adding a dungeon in your house?"

"Well, hopefully this experience will be beneficial," said Mom. "And really bring you two together, like me and my gal." She put her arm around me and squeezed. I beamed up at her.

"Shoot, Dylan's headed for the escalator," said Uncle Max. "I'd better catch him before he gets it going in reverse."

"There's a shuttle van waiting for us!" called Uncle Deke, tapping his watch. "Don't be too long!"

"They'll be fine," said Aunt Zoe. "It's not like they need the money anyway."

I glanced at Angel. Neither of us said anything, but I knew we were both secretly hoping the shuttle would leave without them. If they came along, Dylan would be a huge pain and probably make poor Uncle Max do everything.

But when we reached ground transportation, Dylan and Uncle Max were already there, standing beside a man holding a sign that said ARCHIBALD FAMILY.

"That's them," Uncle Max told the driver, pointing us out.

The man nodded and tucked the sign under one arm.

"This way, please." He gestured for us to follow him to a

shuttle van with an ARCHIBALD FARMS decal on the side.

"Archibald Farms?" I said. "I didn't know Great-Aunt Muriel was a . . . a woman of the land."

I realized I didn't know much about her at all.

"Is that how she got so rich?" asked Angel.

"The second time," said Uncle Deke. "The first time was from steel during World War II."

"She was one of the few respected women in the upper echelons of the business world back then," added Aunt Zoe.

I shook my head. "That doesn't make sense. A woman at her attorney's office said she was in the business of knowing other people's business."

The adults all chuckled.

"I don't doubt it," said Uncle Deke. "Great-Aunt Muriel knew your parents had eloped weeks before anyone else."

Mom smirked. "She was a crafty one. Always one step ahead."

I smiled, picturing Great-Aunt Muriel in her thick rope of pearls, making deals at a table of scowling businessmen. Something told me she had no problem holding her own in that crowd. If she were still alive, I might have actually liked her a little.

"Please watch your heads as you enter the vehicle," said the driver, "and place any belongings that aren't medically necessary in the back." He popped open the rear door. "They'll be returned to you when you leave the contest."

Mom handed over our backpack (we'd eaten the bananas on the plane), and we climbed into the passenger side of the van. Dylan climbed in next, pausing long enough to fart beside my seat before walking back to his.

"Gross!" I screeched, punching him in the arm.

"Get used to it," he said. "That's the smell of victory. *My* victory."

I looked to Mom for help, and she shrugged. "Things are going to smell a lot worse by the end of two weeks."

"If you last that long," said Dylan.

I whirled around to look at him. "Care to make a side bet, smart aleck?"

Dylan snorted. "You want to give me extra money? Sure."

"Not money," I said. "Pride. If you lose, you have to wear one of my mom's dresses on the first day back to school. And I want photographic proof."

Dylan hesitated a second before nodding. "Fine. And if you lose, you have to do my homework for a month. I'll e-mail it. And it'll be *hard*."

"Awww, still can't stack the blocks by yourself?" I asked. "Deal." I extended a hand, and we shook. His fingers were sticky.

He leaned back in his seat. "I'm going to enjoy kicking your butt no matter what the stakes."

"Stakes . . . steaks," said Mom, rubbing her stomach. "Now I'm hungry again."

"Steaks would definitely hit the spot," said Uncle Max with a chuckle.

"Lunch will be waiting when you reach the estate," said the shuttle driver, climbing into his seat.

"Are we the only ones competing?" I asked. If that was the case, the odds weren't looking too bad.

"No, some of the others are already at the property, and the rest arrive tonight." He pulled away from the curb. "Ten families in total."

Dylan fiddled with a monitor and DVD player on the ceiling. "Does this thing get cable?" he asked.

At least there was *one* family I didn't have to worry about.

"Actually, I do have a little something for you to watch," the driver said, reaching back to offer a disc.

I took it and slid it into the player.

Great-Aunt Muriel appeared on-screen, wearing a neck-choking blouse clasped shut with a huge diamond brooch. A frown creased both sides of her face, giving her a bulldoggish appearance.

"Greetings, contestants. I see you've chosen money over self-respect." She narrowed her eyes in what was probably meant to be a disapproving manner but made her appear comical instead.

"Nevertheless," she said, "I applaud your intrepid spirit. Very few people would willingly give up everything to start over with nothing. I should know."

I turned to Mom. "What did she mean by that?"

Uncle Deke paused the video. "Remember how I said she was successful during World War II? After the country started to recover, she suddenly wasn't necessary anymore."

"Because she was a woman," said Aunt Zoe with a disapproving tone. "And they didn't belong in the boardroom unless they were secretaries taking memos."

Dylan laughed. I leaned over and punched him in the leg.

"Anyway," said Uncle Deke, "the only way she would be allowed to stay in business was if she gave up control and became a silent partner. Of course she refused, so the others in her company ruined her and drove her into bankruptcy. She had to sell everything."

"That's so sad," said Angel.

"She survived worse, from what I hear," said Mom. "She grew up during the Great Depression, and her family lived in a Hooverville."

At the confused look on my face, Mom added, "A poor area of town where all the houses are just shacks of scrap wood."

"Really?" I couldn't see Great-Aunt Muriel living in a shack. I could see her maybe bulldozing one to build a stable for her pony, but never living in one.

Uncle Deke restarted the video.

"My groundskeeper and his family await you at the manor. They will be your instructors and judges. Even if you don't win the contest, I hope you leave this experience with more than Lyme disease," said Great-Aunt Muriel. "History has a great deal to teach us if we are willing to learn from it. That being said, I bring you a brief film on colonial life that may come in handy during the contest. Best of luck, and please don't die in my koi pond."

Her image faded and was replaced by a documentary on colonial living. It ended just as the shuttle driver turned onto a dirt road and stopped the van.

"This is as far as I go," he said. "The dirt road will lead you all the way to the manor, and you can either continue on foot or take the wagon . . . once you assemble it."

He pointed to a stack of wheels and tools leaning against a wheelless wagon bed. We all thanked him and climbed out of the van.

"So where do we start?" I asked.

Uncle Max chuckled. "By deciding who's going to pull this thing once it's built!"

As if on cue, there was a whinnying sound from a nearby grove of trees. Dylan walked over to investigate and returned holding the reins of two horses.

"They're not fast, but they'll do," he said, pulling them alongside the wagon bed.

"Actually, they're perfect," said Uncle Max. "We need work horses, not racing ones."

"Not if we want to win!" said Dylan. "Let's go, Dad!"

He jumped atop the wagon bed, and from there leapt onto the back of one of the horses, digging his heels into its sides.

"Dylan!" we all shouted, but he was already galloping toward the manor.

And proving that he was smarter than I thought.

Chapter Four

But he wasn't the only one full of surprises.

Mom swung onto the other horse, shouting, "No you don't!"

The horse reared and gave a terrified whinny, but Mom gripped the reins and took off. A second trail of dust appeared next to Dylan's.

The rest of us stood there, wide-eyed and slack-jawed.

"Did that really just happen?" asked Aunt Zoe. She turned to me. "Your mother, who I've seen fall off a yoga ball, just . . ." She trailed off.

"I know!" I said, still in shock. "She told me she worked at a summer camp. I didn't realize it was Camp Stuntwoman."

"Well, hopefully she'll catch Dylan and we can get out of here," said Uncle Deke.

"Sorry again, folks," said Uncle Max with a chuckle, though it was strained and his face had turned bright red. "I guess my son's more of a go-getter than I thought."

"It's okay." Uncle Deke patted him on the shoulder. "Any of us would have done the same."

None of us would have done the same, but I nodded and said, "Let's put the wagon together so it'll be ready when they come back."

We all set to work with one eye on the wagon and one on the road, and after ten minutes the two horses appeared with only one rider—Mom. She sat atop one while pulling the reins of the other.

Uncle Max frowned and approached her as she slowed her horse to a walk.

"Where's Dylan?" he asked.

"He's fine," said Mom. She passed over both sets of reins and dismounted. "I left him standing next to the road so both horses wouldn't be weighed down. Is the wagon ready?"

"Almost," said Uncle Deke, hammering a wheel onto the

back axle. Uncle Max helped him while Mom and Aunt Zoe hitched the horses to the wagon. Then everyone piled in, and Uncle Max coaxed the team forward.

We moved like snails over gravel.

"Can't this thing go any faster?" asked Angel.

"Sweetheart, if it did, your teeth would rattle out of your head," said Uncle Max. "A contraption like this doesn't have shock absorbers, you know."

"Not to mention the horses are probably tired from running," said Mom. "Just sit back and enjoy the scenery."

I tugged her arm and made her sit beside me.

"What if Dylan's already at the estate setting up booby traps?" I whispered.

"Won't happen," said Mom, pulling her hair into a ponytail.

"I don't know. He was smart enough to hijack a horse."

Mom shook her head. "No, I mean he won't be going anywhere. Trust me."

I narrowed my eyes. "How can you be sure?"

She smiled. "Because we've almost reached the tree I threw his shoes into."

"Ha!" I blurted, then clapped a hand over my mouth. "Mom, I'm pretty sure that's sabotage!" I whispered louder.

Mom blinked at me innocently. "I was trying to knock some

peaches out of the tree, and I needed something to throw," she said with a shrug. "Nobody could argue with that."

The wagon slowed to a standstill, and we poked our heads around the horses.

"I think Dylan could," I said.

Dylan waited under the tree, scowling at us. His cheeks had turned a ruddy pink, and he wore his shirt wrapped around his head like a turban.

"If he crossed his arms, he'd look like a genie." Angel poked me, giggling.

"Yeah," I said, "but I don't think he's going to be granting any wishes."

"Son," said Uncle Max with a raised eyebrow, "where are your shoes?"

"Ask *her*," Dylan snarled, pointing at Mom.

She stood on the driver's seat of the wagon and reached into the tree limbs, extracting a pair of tennis shoes with the laces tied together. Dylan snatched them from her and climbed into the wagon. Nobody said anything, even Uncle Max. He simply shook the reins, and the horses pressed on.

After another ten minutes or so, a butter-colored building with green trim appeared through a break in the trees. It stood a couple of stories tall, with windows spanning six across.

"Is that Archibald Manor?" I asked.

The others shifted forward to get a better look.

"It is indeed," said Uncle Deke.

"It's beautiful," said Angel.

"It's tiny," said Dylan. "I thought mansions were supposed to be huge, with fountains and bushes shaped like things."

"It *was* huge for that time period," said Aunt Zoe. "And the value now is in the fact that it's still standing, as well as whatever antiques it contains."

As we got closer to the trees, I could see that the manor stretched back as far as it did across, with a few smaller buildings behind it.

"What's that?" I asked.

"Please let it be a day spa," Angel whispered.

"I'm guessing servants' quarters," said Uncle Deke.

And sure enough, a woman in a white apron and purple frock stepped out of one of the buildings, toting a basket piled with corn. She waved to us and bustled over.

"Well met, weary travelers," she said, her warm smile reaching her eyes. "You've arrived just in time for dinner."

"Dinner?!" squeaked Dylan. "How long was I standing under that tree?" He shot an accusatory glance at Mom.

"Dinner was the afternoon meal in colonial times," I told

him. "They didn't have lunch. It was breakfast, then dinner, then supper."

"The girl is wise," said the woman with an approving nod. "I am Felicity Hawkins, though you may call me Felicity. What be your names?"

"Tori," I said. "And this is my mom, J—"

"Ah ah!" The woman wagged a finger. "You would simply call her Mother." She turned to Mom. Or rather, *Mother*. "What could I call you, madam?"

Mom cleared her throat. "Jill."

The woman gestured to the others, who introduced themselves. Then she nodded and pointed to the manor's back door. "If you would follow me, dinner awaits."

Resting the basket on her hip, she pushed open the door and stepped inside. We followed single file, and I couldn't help running my fingers along the side of the building, touching a piece of my family's history.

The back door led into a sunken kitchen, which was almost too warm for comfort, thanks to a massive hearth blazing in the corner. But the aroma of roasting meats and vegetables from the hanging pots made my stomach growl.

Felicity climbed a couple of steps and opened another door, where a long table waited, half its chairs already occupied.

The adults greeted one another loudly, and Angel and I hung back, feeling a little shy. Dylan ignored all of us, choosing to hold a burping contest with himself instead.

Our parents introduced us to extended-family members, and I mentally calculated how long each one might last. Quickest to go would probably be Great-Aunt Muriel's daughter, who looked almost as ancient as Great-Aunt Muriel. When people introduced themselves, she nodded and called them by a completely different name.

"Nice to meet you, Dora," she told me.

Next to go would be Sadie and Sam, who were holding a new baby. No way they'd be able to care for someone so little and still keep up. I was debating who would go third, a man who was already dozing at the table or a lady who kept knocking things over, when a tall costumed man approached us.

"Members of the extended Archibald family," he said, "we welcome you to the manor and hope you will enjoy your stay. I am Eli, keeper of the grounds and contest coordinator. After dinner, my son, Caleb, and I will show you around the property and teach you basic skills you'll need to survive these colonial times. Until then, eat, drink, and make merry!"

He clapped his hands loudly, and two younger women appeared with platters of food that they set before us. Roasted beef and chickens, corn on the cob, baked beans and chowder . . .

The table was quiet for several minutes as everyone tucked in to their food. None of us knew when we would eat so well again, so we piled our plates high. Since Angel's family was vegan, I gave her my helping of corn and took her chicken, although it tasted different from how it did back home.

"There's a lot of dark meat on this chicken," I said.

"'Tis not chicken," said Felicity. "'Tis squab, a traditional colonial dish."

"Squab?" I repeated, taking another bite. "I've never heard of that. Are they only around this area?"

"Nay," said Felicity. "They live in your big cities, though you know them by a different name: pigeons."

I instantly choked and started coughing.

"Pigeons?" Angel squeaked, scooting away from my plate as if the contents might take flight.

Even Mom turned a little green.

"Baby pigeons to be exact," said Felicity.

If I hadn't already been hacking up a lung, I would've screamed.

Dylan offered me a mug, smiling. "Warm goat milk to wash down your baby pigeon?"

That was more than I could handle, and I sprinted toward the kitchen for a place to spit it out. But right as I pushed through the door, I smashed into someone and fell, swallowing the squab.

So far, colonial times were disgusting and dangerous.

"Whoa! Are you all right?"

I rolled onto my side, and a cute guy about my age knelt beside me. A cute guy with a capital WOW.

He was wearing a black, triangular hat with only the sides of his dark hair visible. The front point of his hat rested low above eyes the same warm brown as Felicity's.

I must have been staring longer than I thought, because he began snapping his fingers in front of my face.

"Are you with me? What year is it?" he asked.

I blushed and pushed his hand aside. "1680," I said.

He grinned and rocked back onto his heels. "My name's Caleb. What were you running from?" His face took on a serious expression. "And should I be running too?"

I smiled and pointed at the dining room. "Squab. And yes."

He wrinkled his nose. "My mom's secret recipe." He reached into a satchel draped over his shoulder and pulled out a flask. "Here."

I eyed the bottle warily. "If that's goat milk, I'm going to throw up on your shoes."

"Apple cider," he said with a laugh. "Goat milk is nasty."

I drank and took deep breaths.

"The squab's not so bad if you imagine it's chicken," he said.

"My imagination is *not* that powerful," I replied, handing back the flask. "Thanks."

"You know my name, but I don't know yours," he said. "Who are you?"

I blinked up at him. Boys that cute never asked my name. They only asked for quiz answers.

Caleb leaned forward expectantly. "If that question was a stumper, you won't last long here."

I shook my head. "Sorry. I've got squab on the brain. I'm Tori."

For some reason, that made him smile. "Victoria Grace Porter. I've read all about you."

I took a step back. "I feel like I should be running again."

"Oh no!" It was Caleb's turn to blush as he waved his arms in front of him. "It wasn't anything creepy. My parents and I received bios on everyone in the competition so we could figure out where your strengths and weaknesses are."

I raised an eyebrow. "And what were mine?"

Caleb shook his head and wagged a finger. "I can't reveal the specifics, *but* I am impressed that you managed to get yourself banned from a museum for a year."

"If you read it on the Internet, don't believe it," I said. "I only broke into the museum because their Cretaceous period sign was wrong and they wouldn't fix it." I paused and cleared my throat. "I'm not sure which is nerdier: that I did it or that I felt you needed to know it."

Caleb laughed. "If it makes you feel better, I once got detention for correcting a teacher."

"Detention? That's kind of a harsh punishment," I said.

"I may have corrected her over the loudspeaker after I sneaked into the principal's office," he said with a grin.

An extreme nerd. I liked this boy already.

"So, is Caleb your real name or your colonial name?" I asked.

He grinned even broader. "Both. My mom and dad are a little old-fashioned."

"Don't worry, *my* mom is—"

"LALALALALA!" a voice shouted through the door.

"About to be disowned," I finished, rolling my eyes.

Mom stumbled down the kitchen steps with her eyes shut and her fingers in her ears.

"HONEY?" she shouted. "ARE YOU DONE BEING SICK?"

At an odd look from Caleb, I explained, "She can't stand it when people throw up. Once, a toddler puked on her favorite shirt, and she threw it out the window."

Caleb's eyes widened in alarm.

"The shirt!" I quickly amended. "Not the toddler."

I stepped forward and tugged on Mom's arm. She peeked out of one eye, and when she saw I looked perfectly healthy *and* that I was standing next to a guy, she quickly did her best imitation of normal.

"Hey! I'm Tori's mom," she said with a wave and a laugh. "Vomit doesn't scare me. It's just a funny bit we do." She nudged me ever so unsubtly.

I turned to Caleb. "Yes, we're thinking of taking our act on the road."

He fought back a laugh and nodded. "It's good material. I should let you get back to it. Nice *running* into you, Tori," he said with a wink.

As soon as he left the kitchen, Mom elbowed me in the side.

"Forget smallpox, you've caught a different bug!" She batted her eyelashes. "The *love*bug."

"Whatever!" I rolled my eyes, but I could feel my cheeks warming.

"Well, I just came to check on you," she said, pushing my hair back. "Glad you're not in pain."

I frowned. "Pain?"

"From being struck by Cupid's arrow." She started making kissy sounds.

"Stop it!" I said, laughing and pushing her toward the dining room.

Everyone at the table stopped talking and watched us.

"You okay?" asked Angel.

"Perhaps I should have told you it *was* chicken," said Felicity.

"I'm fine," I reassured everyone as I sat back down. "Sorry. Just a little . . . culture shock."

"If you think *you* had culture shock," said Angel, "my mom had to use the bathroom, and instead of toilet paper, there's just a bucket of old corncobs."

"They are quite absorbent," said Felicity.

I choked on my food again, only this time it was from laughter.

"It won't be funny when it happens to you," said Aunt Zoe with a frown.

"I'll be sure to gather some leaves," I said. "Or weave some toilet paper on the loom." I pointed to a wooden contraption in the corner.

"That reminds me . . ." said Eli. He clapped his hands again, and the table grew quiet. "None of you are dressed appropriately for the time, so if you have finished eating, I ask that you visit your bedchambers and change into the clothing provided."

Chairs scraped across the floor as we all left the table and ventured upstairs. Portraits and framed pictures hung along the wall leading to the second floor. Most of them were black and white or sepia-toned, and none of them contained people I recognized. Mom pointed to a black-and-white of a beautiful woman in a slinky dark dress.

"That's Great-Aunt Muriel," she said.

I almost couldn't believe it, but the penetrating gaze in the woman's eyes looked all too familiar.

There were wooden signs fastened to each bedroom doorknob, and Mom stopped in front of one that said PORTER.

She opened the door and we both ooohed.

Even though it was centuries old, the room's original beauty was still imaginable. A fireplace occupied one wall, while a massive canopy bed filled most of the floor space. At the foot of the bed stood a trunk made of canvas and leather.

"What's in the box?" asked Mom.

I lifted the lid and reached inside, holding up a white gown.

"Ghost costumes," she said. "Neat."

"Actually, I think it's a shift," I said. "You know, colonial underwear." I tossed it on the bed and sifted through the trunk. "And some petticoats."

I selected a couple of things and passed a set to Mom, who draped them over her shoulder.

"And what have we here?" She opened a chest of drawers.

"Dresses! And they're so"—she held one up—"ugly."

I pulled a shift over my head. "You saw what Felicity was wearing. What did you expect?"

"I just figured she had bad taste," said Mom, holding a dress against herself. "But apparently we all do."

"Would you throw me one?" I asked, securing the petticoat.

Mom chose a red dress for me. "At least the colors are pretty. I pictured all black. Like the Pilgrims."

"Too expensive," I said, taking the dress from her. "It was cheaper to dye the dresses with berries and flowers."

"Well, aren't you just a fountain of information," said Mom, changing into her own costume.

"It's called reading," I said. "You should try it."

"I have! How else would I have known that it takes fifty containers of ice cream to fill a bathtub?"

"That was the best sundae ever," I said with a smile.

"I still think we could've broken a record," said Mom. "Too bad that hairy bar of soap fell in it."

I made a face. "Seriously? After I just ate a pigeon?"

"Sorry."

We finished getting dressed and tied on our bonnets.

"How do I look?" I asked.

"Ready to win the Miss Colonial America pageant," said Mom, grinning. "Let's see if your future husband approves!"

She hurried out of the bedroom with me on her heels.

"Mom, wait! Don't you dare!"

Angel popped her head out of a bedroom across the hall. "What's going on?"

"Mother-daughter embarrassment hour," I said, studying her face. "Are you wearing eye shadow?"

She shook her head. "Fireplace soot."

"*That* doesn't sound like a bad idea at all," I said.

"Sue me! I don't have access to any of my hair or makeup products." She turned to Mom. "Please don't embarrass your daughter or I'll never hear the end of it."

"Oh, relax," said Mom. "I wouldn't do anything to blow her chances. If anything, I *boost* her attraction factor."

"Creepy thoughts should stay in our heads," I reminded her. "Besides, we need to keep our eyes on the prize."

No sooner had I said this than Caleb appeared at the foot of the stairs, talking to one of my relatives. He glanced up and smiled when he caught me looking. I would've tumbled the rest of the way down if Mom hadn't grabbed the back of my dress.

"Something tells me," she whispered, "that we have different ideas of what the prize is."

Chapter Five

Great-Aunt Muriel's estate was even more enormous than I thought. In groups of ten, Eli led us to the highest viewpoint, a widow's walk on the manor's rooftop.

"You've seen the servants' quarters," he said, pointing to the buildings behind the manor. "Beyond the cherry trees to the right are the barn, chicken coop, vegetable garden, and physic garden."

Dylan snorted. "Physic? Pretty sure you mean psychic."

I turned to him. "'Physic' is an older term for medicinal plants, dummy. What the heck would a psychic garden be?"

Dylan blinked at me. "Where gypsies grow their tea leaves."

Eli cleared his throat. "Farther afield be the corn rows and the fruit orchard."

Angel leaned over the railing of the widow's walk and pointed to the left of the manor. "What's that?"

We all looked at a line of barren ground interspersed with straw-filled circles of stone.

"That," said Eli with a grin, "will be your first lesson."

We followed him back to ground level, where he motioned for the rest of the family members to follow to the barren expanse. In under one minute, he'd struck a fire, and in under two he'd lit a torch and was waving it around.

"Fire," he said, "is one of the most important things a colonist can have."

"Fire represents life," whispered Mom.

"You watch too much *Survivor*," I whispered back.

"Fire gives you heat, light, a way to cook food, and a way to protect yourself from predators," Eli continued. "Luckily, the colonists had already discovered *this*." He held out a tan rock.

"Actually, I think cavemen discovered those," said Angel.

"Perhaps," said Eli with a smile. "But they didn't know what was inside."

He placed the rock on a tree stump and struck it with a

sledgehammer, shattering it to pieces. Then he picked one up and pointed at the dark-gray interior. "Flint. Strike this with steel, you get sparks. Let the sparks settle on dry grass, you get fire."

Motioning for us to follow, he crouched beside one of the stone circles where a knife and polished piece of flint were also waiting. He repeated his instructions and demonstrated on the straw, blowing on the sparks to ignite a fire.

"In less than five minutes, half your worldly problems are solved," he said.

Mom turned to me. "He's right, you know. If we caught the dress shop on fire, we wouldn't have to worry about it anymore."

I shushed her.

"I'd like you all to try lighting a fire at least twice," said Eli. "My son, Caleb, and I will be walking around to assist."

At the mention of Caleb, my stomach fluttered, but I kept my face emotionless. The last thing I needed was Mom's relentless teasing. Instead, I chose one of the stations and went to work striking a knife against the flint.

"Watch your fingers," said Mom. "I'm pretty sure if you lose one, the colonial cure is to chop off the rest."

"Your grasp of history is terrifying," I told her, making sparks fly. "Get ready to fan the flames."

"Got it," said Mom, getting down on all fours.

I struck the flint several times until a large spark landed in the straw. Mom took a deep breath and blew with all her might. The straw scattered everywhere.

"Not so hard, Big Bad Wolf!" I said, scooping it back into a pile. "You're not evicting the Three Little Pigs."

"Oh, blah." Mom took the flint and knife. "I'll make the sparks, and *you* blow on the fire with all that hot air you've got stored up."

She struck the flint once, and several sparks settled on the straw. I puckered my lips and barely breathed on the sparks. More rained down around me, and I jumped back.

"*What* are you *doing*?!" I shouted, batting at my hair to make sure *I* hadn't been sent alight.

"You weren't going to get any life out of those little sparks," she said. "You needed more."

"So you thought you'd start a fire on my *head*?"

"Calm down," said Mom. "I would've put it out before it reached your scalp."

I continued to tousle my hair, certain I smelled something burning. "You can be such a—"

"Caleb," said Mom.

"No," I said. "Such a *pain*."

"No." Mom grabbed my shoulders and spun me around.

Caleb was staring right at me. Me and my now-snaggled poufy do.

I froze with hands in my hair like a baboon.

Caleb sauntered over with an amused grin. "You two are the loudest fire starters I've ever seen," he said. "Minus the fire. Show me your technique."

Mom placed the flint close to the straw, not my *head*, and struck it while I blew on the sparks.

"That's pretty good," said Caleb. "But let me show you how it might work better."

He demonstrated, making smoke curl up before sprinkling it with dirt to extinguish it.

"Now you try."

Mom and I did until, lo and behold, a tiny wisp of smoke climbed skyward.

"Woohoo!" I shouted. Unfortunately, I was still lying right beside the pile of straw, and our speck of a fire went out.

I refused to glance in Mom's direction.

She cleared her throat. "Thanks for the help, Caleb. I'm sure Typhoon Tori and I can manage from here."

He laughed. "Everyone gets excited about their first fire. Don't blame her."

I continued to lie where I was, blushing. "Thanks, Caleb."

He nodded and smiled. "I'll see you around, Tori," he said, walking off to help someone else.

Mom nudged me. "He came to your defense," she whispered. "So knight-in-shining-armor!"

"I guess," I said with an eye roll. But my insides were doing a happy dance. "Let's get this fire started." I didn't want to make Caleb feel like he'd wasted his time.

Instead of hunkering down, Mom stood up and brushed off her dress.

"You work on the fire while I check out the competition," she said.

I goggled at her. "Are you serious? We shouldn't even care how they're doing until we can build ours."

"I have faith in you. Besides," Mom said with a wink, "if you mess up, it'll give Caleb an excuse to come by."

I mulled this over. "Maybe you should check out the competition."

Mom grinned. "Be back soon."

At the station beside ours, Dylan and Uncle Max already had a nice fire going. When Dylan saw me looking, he inclined his head and threw his arms open wide.

"Who's the champ?" he bellowed.

"More like 'who's the chimp?'" I muttered, returning to my fire.

While I battled with the flint, an Angel-shaped shadow blocked out the sun.

"Please tell me you're burning an offering to the god who destroys boy cousins."

"Lord Dylan Killer?" I asked with a smirk. "No, I'm actually trying to start a fire."

Angel kicked at the pile of straw. "Haven't you had enough practice? How many fires have you made already?"

I rocked back onto my heels. "To me, it's more about getting a *feel*—"

"So, zero."

"Yeah, we may have set civilization back a thousand years." I swiped at the flint with my knife. "I don't get how this can be so difficult."

"Use the filings." Angel borrowed my flint, but instead of striking it, she used the blade to saw off silvery dust that coated the hay. "Try it now."

I gave her a dubious look but did so, creating sparks and . . . fire!

Being careful not to shout it out of existence, I bent low and coaxed the flame to life with my breath.

"Ta-da!" said Angel.

"That's amazing," I said, watching the straw shrivel and

brown under the extreme heat. "Why didn't Caleb mention it?"

"Because he probably doesn't watch YouTube," said Angel with a smirk. "Like I said, I did a little research before we got here."

"Well, thanks," I said. "And if there's anything I can help you with, just name it."

She leaned closer. "Let's just make sure Dylan doesn't win the whole thing."

We both turned to look at our cousin, who had a roaring fire going and had barbecued *something* over it. He cackled evilly and waved it at us.

"I guess this rabbit didn't have *any* lucky feet!" he said.

Angel gasped and shielded her eyes.

"It's probably not a real rabbit," I assured her. "We would've smelled burning fur. . . ." I trailed off at the horrified expression on her face.

"I have to go inside," she whispered, nearly colliding with Mom as she made her escape.

"Angel, honey, you okay?" Mom called after her. She turned to me with a frown. "What's up with her? And Dylan, why are you cooking your socks?"

For the first time, I noticed his bare feet and rolled my eyes. "I *told* her it wasn't rabbit."

Dylan cackled again and turned away.

"Huh?" Mom's forehead wrinkled but quickly ironed out when she spotted our fire.

"You did it!" She hugged me.

"Well, Angel helped," I said, placing a couple of random twigs on the fire. "But I think I can manage from now on. What did you learn on your little scouting mission?"

Mom sat beside me. "Well, apparently Great-Cousin Meg and her husband have a nanny who steals from them, and Half-Cousin Jeff has a *liiittle* bit of a gambling problem, which—"

I put a hand on her arm. "What did you learn about their competitive skills?" I amended.

"Oh!" Mom tilted her hand from side to side. "Right now, I'd say we have a pretty good chance against almost everyone. Step-Niece Tamara can get a fire going quick, but since she's *afraid* of them, she immediately screams and puts it out."

"She's afraid of fire?" I repeated. "What is she, a scarecrow?"

"She's also afraid of heights and pushy salespeople," said Mom.

"Hmm." I poked at the fire. "Maybe we can use that to our advantage."

Mom stared at me. "How, darling? Take her to the roof and try to sell her a car?"

"You said we have a pretty good chance against *almost*

everyone," I said. "I'm guessing Angel's family and Dylan and Uncle Max are the real competition."

"Bingo." Mom fired a finger gun at me. "Dylan doesn't act very bright, but he has moments that make me wonder if that's all it is—just an act."

I looked past Mom to where Dylan and Max's fire station had been. All that remained was a smoldering pile of ash and a stick holding two barbecued socks.

"You should put out that fire," said Mom, nudging me. "We have some more tasks to learn before supper."

Since it was a small fire, I grabbed a cup of water sitting on the ground and splashed it onto the flames. They shot up higher, and I squealed. Mom yanked me back and kicked dirt at the base, smothering the flames.

"What was *that*?" she demanded.

I lifted the cup and sniffed. A strong odor of kerosene made me cough and gag. "Gas!"

"How can that be?" she asked.

"I'll give you one guess," I said.

I went in search of a faucet for some actual water to wash my hands. Instead, I found Caleb.

"Hey, I saw that fire you had going!" he told me. "Nice job!"

"Thanks," I said, smiling. I decided not to mention just how big it got. "Filing off some of the flint helped."

He nodded. "I didn't want to suggest it, since you only get once piece to last the whole time you're here, but that's a quick way to do it." He eyed my hands. "If you're trying to clean up, we have a pump by the servants' quarters."

I followed him, and he rolled up his sleeves to get the pump going. While I ducked my hands under the water, he worked the handle. Something on his wrist glinted in the sunlight.

"I didn't know colonial men wore bracelets," I said, wiping my hands on my dress.

"A few did," said Caleb. "But this is more a family pride thing." He held the bracelet out for my inspection. It was a piece of black braided leather with a strip of copper attached in the middle. The initials *PR* were stamped in the copper.

"This reminds me of my dad," I said, touching the outline. I explained about his flattened-coin collection. "What do the initials stand for?"

"Paul Revere," said Caleb. "He's one of my ancestors."

"Paul Revere?" I gawked at him. "*The* Paul Revere? As in 'The British are coming!'?"

"So you've heard of him," said Caleb with a grin. "Most girls aren't impressed by that."

I made a face. "Well, I think we established I'm a bit of a nerd, so . . ."

"I like it," said Caleb.

"Oh." My cheeks warmed. "Cool. So . . . uh . . . where did you get the bracelet?"

"I made it," he said, a hint of pride in his voice. "If you want, I can show you, and you can make one with your dad's initials."

A broad smile crossed my face. "I'd love that."

Caleb smiled back. "Great!" he said. "Can you meet me here after supper, or will you be busy?"

"It's the imaginary 1600s," I said. "What would I be busy doing?"

"I don't know." Caleb scratched his head and grinned. "That fire took an *awful* lot of your time."

"Hey!" I playfully pushed him.

He held his hands up in surrender. "Okay, okay. Since it won't take you *any* time at all to start a fire, I'll expect to see you here after the canary pudding."

I made a face. "And I will be here *before* the canary pudding."

Caleb laughed. "It's made with lemons, not birds. I promise."

Eli whistled for all of us to gather around to learn a new skill, but I was only half listening. I wasn't sure what made me more nervous . . . canary pudding or a kind-of, maybe date with Caleb.

❄

"Because that's what it is, right? A date?" I asked Mom later. We were up in our room, sprawled across the bed as comfortably as our gowns would allow. I'd just filled her in on my conversation with Caleb.

"I'm not sure," she said with a frown. "I've never dated a colonial gentleman. I guess it depends on if he offers you a bouquet of corn and polishes his shoe buckles."

I rolled my eyes. "He didn't ask Angel as far as I know, so it might be a date. *But* it could just be because I admired his bracelet."

Mom patted my leg. "Yes, honey, that's it. He's interested in you because you have the same taste in jewelry."

I propped myself up on my elbows. "So it *is* a date."

Mom groaned and rubbed her temples. "Does it really matter?"

"I need to know. How I act will depend on whether or not we're just friends or something more."

"Why don't you quit worrying so much and just enjoy it?" asked Mom. "Live for the moment."

"Says the woman who freaked when Funk saw her in a bathrobe."

Mom popped me across the face with a pillow.

"You're lucky I can barely move in this dress or I'd get you back," I said. "I think my sweat made it extra starchy."

She leaned toward me and wrinkled her nose. "It made it extra *something*, anyway."

"What?" I ducked my head into an armpit. "Whoa!"

In the ripeness category, I could definitely give Dylan a run for his money.

"I need deodorant," I said, getting off the bed and heading for the bathroom door.

"Um . . . Tori? Slight problem!" Mom called after me.

I stopped halfway and whirled to face her. "We don't *have* deodorant!" I gasped. "And I have to meet Caleb after canary pudding!"

Mom frowned. "I've been meaning to ask you about that. Do the canaries *make* the pudding, or . . ."

I grabbed Mom by the shoulders. "Focus! What do I do?"

"Take a shower and try to not lift your arms," she said.

I turned my back to her. "Here. Untie me so I can wash off this stink."

Mom helped me out of the dress, and I made a beeline for the bathroom. Inside was a large copper tub. And no plumbing attached.

"Looks like you have to smell worse before you can smell better," said Mom, picking up an empty bucket and holding it out.

I sighed. "Forget it. I saw some roses on the nightstand. I'll just rub them under my arms."

"Or maybe you could give Caleb a bloody nose," said Mom. "That'll keep him stopped up for days."

"You do realize I will never take any of these 'brilliant' ideas of yours seriously?" I asked.

"You took graveyard hide-and-seek seriously," said Mom. "And if I recall, you enjoyed it."

She had me there.

"At least now I get why colonial women always walked around with bunches of flowers," I said, selecting a few roses from the vase. "So they could bury their noses and avoid the stink of civilization."

I swiped a few handfuls of petals under my arms and turned to see Mom doing lunges.

"*What* are you up to?" I asked. "Nobody can see your legs in that dress."

"Well," said Mom, huffing with each drop, "I figured that if I sweat like crazy and maximize *my* BO, you'll smell better by comparison."

I smiled at her. "Awww. Really? That's disgusting but sweet!"

Mom winked at me and breathed deep. Then she coughed. "Yep. I'd say I'm almost there."

Ten minutes later, we joined everyone for dinner, smelling of roses and rankness. If anyone noticed, they were polite enough not to say anything, although Angel's nostrils twitched when I sat beside her.

"Be honest," I whispered. "Do I stink?"

Angel reached for a plate of grilled leeks. "Not if I don't breathe."

"Perfect." I pressed my arms against my sides. "Would you mind passing the ham?"

"You want me, a vegan, to hand you a platter of chopped-up pig?" she asked.

"Or I could reach across you and get it myself," I said, lifting my arms.

Angel jumped into action and even slid several slices of ham onto my plate.

"Anything else?" she asked. "Some more pigeon, perhaps?"

I gave her a withering look. "Just some vegetables, thanks."

She scooped them onto my plate, and I did my best to eat with my arms tucked against my chest.

"You look like a *Tyrannosaurus rex*," she said. "And you don't actually smell *that* bad. Not compared to your mom anyway."

I snickered. "The things she does for love."

"What?" Angel leaned back in her chair and looked around. "Funk is here?"

"No! *Me*." I explained about Caleb, and Angel batted her eyelashes and pursed her lips.

"So sweet. But since he's from colonial times, is your mom okay with you dating a 340-year-old?"

"Ha!" I pointed at her. "So it *is* a date!"

"Sounds like it to me," said Angel. "I wasn't invited, and I smell *way* better than you."

"That settles it." I scarfed down my ham and left my vegetables behind. "I have *got* to take a bath."

"Good luck. There's no running water," said Angel.

"No," I said. "But there *is* some water in the kitchen that someone set aside for coffee."

I checked to make sure everyone was still engaged in dinner, then crept into the kitchen. Several pails of water sat next to the open hearth, waiting to be boiled. Surely nobody would miss *one*.

I hoisted a pail in one hand and grabbed a scrap of soap from a shelf of cleaning supplies. Then I snuck through a side door and up the stairs to the bathroom. It was the coldest, quickest bath I'd ever had, and the soap wasn't exactly supermarket quality, but it took away the stench.

The clothes were another matter.

Luckily, in the wardrobe was one more dress each for Mom

and me. I had a feeling it was supposed to wait until next week, but desperate times called for desperate measures.

I ran my fingers through my hair and checked my reflection in a mirror before creeping back downstairs. From the looks of things, everyone was finishing dessert, and the place at the table where Caleb sat was empty. My heart beat a little faster as I brushed past Mom and squeezed her shoulder before heading outside.

Caleb was standing next to the water pump and smiled when he saw me. I returned his smile and walked a little faster.

"You came!" he said. "We were wondering what happened to you."

"We?" I stopped in my tracks as Dylan stepped out of the shadows beside Caleb.

Nope. This was definitely *not* a date.

Chapter Six

"Family fun time," I said with a forced smile. "Neat."

Caleb cringed and shrugged. "Your cousin heard us talking, and apparently he's really into making things with his hands."

I rolled my eyes. "Please. The only thing he's ever made with his hands is a fart trap."

"Any guesses about the catch of the day?" asked Dylan, holding out his cupped palm.

Caleb wrinkled his nose and stepped back. "Let's just head to the craft hut."

He led the way to a tiny shack I hadn't noticed on the opposite side of the manor. Outside it was planked wood, but the walls inside were a mix of woven wicker and cement.

"Wattle and daub," Caleb corrected me when I mentioned it. "The wattle is the wood strips woven together, and the daub is the filler."

I scratched at it with a fingernail. "Mud?"

"And horse droppings."

My hand snapped back.

Caleb grinned, watching me wipe my fingers on my dress. "I probably shouldn't tell you what you'll be starting most fires with. And that is where the magic happens."

He nodded to a glowing coal pit against one wall, and I realized just how warm it was in the room. Several deep clangs sounded beside us, and we spun around. Dylan had picked up a hammer and was striking a row of hanging metal discs, one after the other.

"Ladies and gentlemen, Dylan the Destroyer on drums!" he shouted to an imaginary crowd.

"Don't!" Caleb snatched the hammer away. "Nobody's going to buy those plates if they're warped."

"Nobody's going to buy them anyway," said Dylan, pulling one off its hook. "They're too dirty to eat off of."

"They're not for holding food," said Caleb. "They're decorative."

"Really?" Dylan held the plate up to the light. "Who would decorate with this? A blind guy?"

This time, I snatched away what was in his hands. "Obviously, it's not finished yet." I turned to Caleb. "Is it?"

He shook his head, then blushed. "But if you want, I can show you what I'm working on."

I smiled. "Sure!"

"I'll pass," said Dylan. "When can I make my armor?"

Caleb raised an eyebrow. "We're making bracelets, Dylan."

"Bracelets are for wusses." Dylan picked up a knobbed handle with a sharp needle attached. "What's this?"

"An awl," said Caleb. "It's used for punching leather."

"And maybe people?" Dylan turned toward me and reeled back the fist clutching the awl. I smacked him in the face with the metal plate.

"Owww!" he cried, dropping the awl and rubbing his nose.

I handed the plate over to Caleb. "Warped metal meets warped cousin."

He examined the disc. "Actually, other than the greasy face print, it looks okay."

"I think my nose is broken!" said Dylan.

"You weren't using it for anything besides a finger warmer anyway," I said, but inspected his face. "You're fine." Then I turned to Caleb. "So, what are you working on?"

He grabbed a sketchbook off a worktable and showed me the contents. "Family crests."

"These are awesome!" I said, flipping the pages. "And you can do this on metal?"

"Of course," he said. "Watch."

Caleb approached the fire pit and reached to one side, picking up a bellows and pointing the nozzle at the coals. With a few squeezes, he managed to shoot enough air onto the coals to reignite a small flame.

"All right!" said Dylan. "Armor time!"

Caleb fished a scrap of metal out of his pocket and tossed it to Dylan. "Here's what you have to work with. Maybe you can make a pinky shield."

He fished another scrap of metal out of his pocket and placed it between two tongs.

"Before we can engrave anything on the metal, we have to flatten it," he told me, pushing the tongs directly into the coals. "And before we can flatten it, we have to heat the metal to a bending point."

When the metal was glowing bright orange, Caleb removed the tongs from the fire and rested the scrap on an anvil. Then he took the hammer that Dylan had been using and struck the metal, making sparks fly. After a few hits, he offered the hammer to me.

"Want to try?"

I took it and hoisted the hammer over one shoulder, bringing it down hard on the metal.

Which promptly split in half.

"Shoot," I said.

"Ha!" Dylan said.

"Careful," Caleb said. "You're trying to flatten the surface, not destroy the One Ring." He took another piece of metal from his pocket and held it up. "Let's try again. And this time, hammer from here."

He wrapped a hand around mine and lowered my arm down by my side, making a less violent swinging gesture. Even though it was a billion degrees in the hut, Caleb's hand felt even warmer on mine.

"Yep," I squeaked, and cleared my throat. "Got it."

He stepped back, and I almost stepped back too, just to keep the closeness between us. But when I glanced up, Dylan was watching with a measured stare.

On my second attempt, I was able to hammer the metal flat, and then Dylan took a turn with his piece. Caleb showed us how to use a hammer and graver to etch the metal and then pierced the sides so we could run leather strips through them.

When we left the craft hut, Caleb shook both our hands, but it felt like he held on to mine a little longer. Or . . . at least I liked to think so.

As soon as Dylan and I were back in the house, I faced him and scowled.

"I know you have no interest in making bracelets," I said. "So why did you—"

"Crash your little 'date'?" he asked with a smirk. "Your mom stole my shoes. And I'm the vengeful type."

"Yeah?" I crossed my arms. "The fire wasn't enough?"

"Chicks are too sensitive," he scoffed.

I scanned his face. "I think your nose looks a little flatter since I smashed it. Try not to snore and wake your dad."

I headed up to the room that Mom and I were sharing and found her sitting on the floor with a ball of yarn.

"Please tell me we have an invisible cat and it's not just you batting that thing around," I said.

"Don't mock." She waggled a finger at me. "Without electricity or books or *you*, this was the only thing I could find to entertain myself. I came up with two games. Roll the Yarn and Stare at the Yarn." She bounced to her feet and smiled. "But now you're back to tell me about your exciting date!" She nudged the yarn away with her toe.

"Hey, look at that," I said. "Kick the Yarn. And my exciting date . . . wasn't."

Mom grimaced. "He turned out to be a bore, huh?"

"No, he was fine," I said, sitting on the edge of the bed. "Dylan was not."

"Say what now?" Mom raised her eyebrows.

I told her about the evening, and Mom just shook her head.

"On the plus side, I have a cool new bracelet." I held it up, and she smiled.

"Your dad's initials." Mom leaned over and kissed the top of my head. "If only he could've seen the amazing creation you turned out to be."

She scooted off the bed and opened the trunk. "What nightgown do you want? Not-so-pretty in pink? Or garish gray?"

"Depends." I wrinkled my nose. "What makes it gray?"

Mom lifted the gown and took a whiff. "Smells clean."

I took it from her warily. "I've seen you apply the same sniff test to clothes on your bedroom floor."

I switched into the nightgown but couldn't quite jump into bed.

"I can't brush my teeth." I ran my tongue over them. "And I really need to."

"Rub them clean on your nightgown," Mom said, demonstrating with the hem of hers.

"Gross! Stop it!" I smacked the cloth out of her hand. "You don't know who died in that thing."

I picked up my modern-day street clothes and used my T-shirt instead. "So why didn't you hang out with Aunt Zoe instead of the yarn?" I asked as I cleaned.

Despite my warning, Mom put the nightgown back in her mouth. "They all went to bed early. Something about breakfast."

"Ugh. Porridge," I said. "Well, at least there're no weird ingredients."

I draped my shirt over a towel rack in the bathroom and climbed into one side of the bed.

"Tomorrow's our first official contest day," I said. "Are you ready?"

"Sure," said Mom, snuffing the candles around the room. "We can handle whatever they throw at us."

Except, as it turned out, waking up at the crack of dawn.

It felt like my eyes had been closed for just a few seconds when someone banged on our door and threw it open.

"Wake up, lazy layabouts!" Eli boomed.

I sucked in a sharp breath and scampered backward,

disoriented, until I was against the wall. Mom continued to snore beside me.

"What time is it?" I asked. The only light came from the hallway.

"Time for you to be downstairs working!" Eli shot back. "Ten minutes or home you go."

He backed out of the room, slamming the door, and a moment later I heard him rousing someone else. I turned to Mom and shook her.

"Wake up! We have to move."

Mom shoved my face away and rolled over. "The roaches are more afraid of you than you are of them," she mumbled.

"Mom!" I shook her again. "We're not at home. We're in Massachusetts."

She didn't say anything.

"Mom." I leaned closer. "Funk is downstairs."

Her eyes shot open. "What?" She threw back the bedsheets and sat up, wild haired. "He can't see me in this gown that doubles as a toothbrush!"

Mom jumped out of bed and promptly collided with something. She muttered a string of words that definitely weren't colonial or ladylike.

"Mom!" I called out. "Funk's not really here. I just wanted to wake you."

There was silence and then . . .

"Geez, Tori!" she shouted, and smacked into something else. "Where the heck is the light switch?"

"There isn't any power," I said to the darkness. "Remember? Colonial times? You snuffed out all the candles last night."

"Because I thought we'd be up after the sun," Mom growled. "Not before it!"

I drew back the curtains, which helped some.

"Open the bedroom door," I told Mom. "There're lights on in the hallway."

She did so, and instantly everything was illuminated.

"Now I'm guessing we have about five minutes," I said, grabbing my alternate dress out of the wardrobe and changing into it. Mom did the same, and we both calmed our hair with our fingers before sprinting downstairs.

Thankfully we weren't the only ones who looked shell shocked, and after I did a quick headcount there was one couple missing. Angel and her parents, though, were already seated at the dining table, sipping from clay mugs.

"Mint tea?" asked Angel, offering hers.

"No, thanks. Room service already brought some up," I said.

Eli paced the floor and stared at a candle on the center of the table.

"The wax drips past the final minute," he said. "And not all parties are present."

There was a thundering of footsteps on the floor above, and two people appeared on the landing, out of breath and disheveled.

"Hasten not your footfalls," said Eli. "You no longer have involvement in this contest."

The couple slumped in unison.

"But—" one of them said.

"Prepare your things for the journey home." Eli turned his back to them and faced us. "The rest of you will notice no meal awaits. We will no longer feed you but will provide instruction so you may feed yourself."

"Teach a man to fish . . . ," said Uncle Max.

"In fact, teach a man to make porridge," said Eli. "Your first challenge: to cook an acceptable gruel to be judged by myself and my kin." He gestured to his wife and Caleb, who stepped forward holding a stack of yellowed paper. I ducked behind Mom.

"Here are your instructions," Caleb said, not even bothering with an accent. "Since there're so many people, everything you need is set up outside."

"You have until the sun rises. Good luck," chimed in Felicity.

We all approached Caleb for our instructions, except me.

"I look like I got dressed in the dark," I whispered to Mom.

"You did," Mom whispered back.

"Well, I can't let Caleb see me like this. Grab the instructions and meet me outside."

I crouched and made a beeline for the kitchen door. Ten different fires were blazing, so there was plenty of light to see by, and over each fire hung a large pot. Beside each fire stood a table with what I assumed were the ingredients to make porridge. I chose a station and studied what was on the table: six dried ears of corn, a bowl of sugar, a wooden spoon, a knife, a mortar and pestle, and a bucket.

"Oh, this already looks delicious," I said.

Mom walked over with the recipe and held it up to the light of our fire.

"Looks like we need to turn this corn into cornmeal, find a milk source, and find a water source."

"There's a water pump by the servants' quarters," I said. "And I think there are some cows in the barn."

Mom nodded and reached for the bucket. "I'll milk the cow and get the water while you grind the cornmeal."

Considering Mom usually bought our chicken in the canned-food aisle, I couldn't help feeling impressed at how quickly she'd come up with an action plan.

Grabbing an ear of corn and the knife, I sawed off the kernels and scooped a few into the mortar. Then I squashed them with the pestle and pushed them around the container until a layer of white powder appeared. I poured the powder into the extra bowl and grabbed another handful of kernels.

By the time I'd filled the bowl, both of my arms ached from turns at the grinder, and I realized Mom hadn't come back yet with the water. I decided to take a break and wandered over to Angel's table.

"Hey!" she said.

"Hey, how's it . . ." I looked past her to her table. "No way."

Her corncobs were gone, her bowl of sugar was gone, and something was bubbling in the pot over the fire. Aunt Zoe gave it a stir with the spoon and smiled at me.

"It's a little thick, I know, but we didn't want any of the bowls of cornmeal to go to waste."

"Bowls . . . plural?" I repeated, glancing at the single bowlful on Mom's and my table.

"Think fast!" said Uncle Deke, tossing me an ear of corn. "We had an extra."

"Oh, Deke, she's probably already done if she's over here visiting," said Aunt Zoe with a chuckle. "How did yours turn out, sweetheart?"

"Mine?" I repeated. "Well, when *I'm* making porridge . . ."

"You're not done," said Angel.

"Not even close." I pressed my lips together and looked at the sky, which was starting to lighten. "I should find my mom."

"Good idea," said Aunt Zoe with a frown.

I could see from where I stood that Mom wasn't at the water pump, so I headed for the barn. Where I found her snuggling with a cow in one of the stalls, fast asleep.

The milk bucket was completely empty.

"Are you kidding me?! Mom!" I shouted, startling the cow to its feet. It dumped Mom on the ground, and she glanced around in confusion.

"Wha . . .?" She rubbed her eyes and then widened them once she saw the bucket. "Oh . . . *no*."

"The sun's almost up!" I grabbed the bucket and crouched next to the cow. "Where are the milk dispensers?"

"This is a male. They don't tend to do that." Mom took the bucket and entered another stall. The cow there stared at me remorsefully while Mom milked it.

"How could you fall asleep?" I asked.

"I guess I'm just . . ." Mom yawned. "Not used to being up so early. Sorry."

She walked back around with the bucket and helped me to my feet. "Let's go fetch that water."

"We don't have another bucket," I said. "You were supposed

to get the water so we could boil it and *then* get the milk."

We had to pump the water directly into the milk, which I had a feeling was a bad idea, but the sky was turning orange, so we couldn't afford to be picky.

"How'd the corn grinding go?" asked Mom as we walked back to our table.

"I filled an entire bowl with cornmeal," I said. "*And* didn't take a break until after I was done." I shook Uncle Deke's ear of corn at her, but she ignored me.

"Sweetheart . . . I don't want to be a pessimist," said Mom, "but that bowl looks more than half-empty. Like . . . completely empty."

"Huh?" I looked to where she was pointing and gasped. "No! It was full! I swear it!" I ran to the table and picked up the bowl. "See? It still has some residue left!"

I ducked my head under the table and gasped even louder. "Someone dumped it!"

"Maybe it fell," said Mom.

"No!" I stood up straight, feeling an angry heat in my cheeks. "If it fell, there'd be a single pile, but someone deliberately poured it out and mixed it in with the dirt so it's unusable."

We both looked in the direction of Dylan and Uncle Max's table. Uncle Max was taste testing the porridge, but Dylan stared straight at us and smiled, rubbing his nose ever so slightly.

This must have been his revenge for a plate to the face.

"We have to tell Eli!" I said to Mom.

She shook her head. "We can't prove it was deliberate. Let's just focus on doing what we can with what we have." Mom poured the water and milk mixture into the pot. "Get the kernels off that ear of corn and I'll grind them."

I sawed at the corn with ragged, angry strokes. "This wouldn't have happened if you'd come back with the water and milk on your own. I never would've—"

"Don't start, Tori." Mom stirred the liquid with a spoon and poured in the sugar. "I already apologized."

She passed the spoon to me and started grinding the corn, although as angry as I felt, I probably could have pulverized the entire ear in five seconds flat.

Eli strolled by and peered into our simmering pot. "Your porridge seems watery."

"That's because it *is* water," I snapped.

"Manners, Tori!" Mom shouted in a harsh voice I'd never heard her use before.

I instantly clammed up and stirred the pot.

"We had some . . . technical difficulties," Mom told Eli. She put down the pestle and poured the contents of the mortar into the pot. "But we're fine now."

Eli nodded. "Good. Because you have roughly"—he gazed at the sky—"fifteen stirs of the spoon before sunrise."

"What if I stir really slow?" I asked.

Mom gave me another look, but Eli laughed and continued to another table.

I stirred the porridge until Eli called time, then scooped a little to study it.

"I'm not a psychic, but I'm pretty sure we aren't going to score high on this challenge," I said.

And we didn't.

Angel and her family scored the highest, Dylan and Uncle Max scored somewhere in the middle, and Mom and I came in dead last. Apparently, our porridge was too sweet, too watery, too chunky, and had an acorn in it.

"Heh. It's just like a cereal-box prize," said Mom, plucking it off Eli's spoon.

When the results were announced, I groaned and buried my head in my hands. Mom hugged me close.

"So we're not off to a strong start," she said. "But we'll rally and win this whole thing."

I nodded into her shoulder but didn't say what I was thinking.

That I'd need to be a team of one for that to happen.

Chapter Seven

In colonial times, families of a village would help each other out in moments of need. Like when a girl was starving because all she'd had for breakfast was four spoonfuls of porridge soup.

But since this was modern times and an elimination contest, nobody was interested in sharing their gruel with me and Mom. Not even Angel.

"Sorry," she said, "but we need all the strength we can get." She ran her spoon around the edge of the bowl, scooping out the last grains of porridge.

"Uh-huh," I said, drooling a little. "Are you gonna eat the drop that fell on your shoe?"

Angel crinkled her nose. "You need to start watching out for Dylan. He's singling you out for some reason. Play smarter."

"I'm playing smart enough," I said defensively. "I just didn't expect him to be so malicious and evil."

"We must be talking about Dylan," said Mom, walking over with something fuzzy in each hand. She tossed me one. "Heads up! As usual, your mother comes through in a pinch."

I grabbed the peach midair and frowned at it. "Hmm. No real protein." I took a huge bite anyway, chewing slowly and savoring the taste of something other than the air I'd been swallowing. "Where did you get these?"

"Oh, there's a Trader Joe's behind the cornfield," Mom said with a casual wave of her hand. "Where do you think I got them? I found a peach tree."

"Did you also find a bacon-sandwich tree?" I asked. "Or a tree that eats evil boys? Because I could take a stroll with Dylan after breakfast."

Mom shook her head. "I can't figure out how someone like that could come from someone like . . ." She nodded at Uncle Max.

"Maybe he gets the evil from his mom's side," said Angel.

I rolled my eyes. "It's not like bad habits are hereditary.

Otherwise I would've been sleeping in the barn right along-side her." I poked Mom in the side and she grabbed my finger, twisting my arm behind my back.

"Say 'My mom is the best mom in the world!'" she said, tickling my side.

I laughed and squirmed. "I can't! You taught me never to lie!"

Angel smiled at the two of us but then quickly sobered and straightened up.

"Eli," she whispered.

Mom and I disentangled ourselves from one another and stood side by side.

Eli placed his hands behind his back and stopped in front of me and Mom.

"It pleaseth me your spirits remain high despite earlier troubles," he said. "I hope the tasks of your day prove not overwhelming in nature."

"Tasks of the day?" I repeated. "What would those be?"

Eli clucked his tongue. "If you cannot suss what needs be done, yours will be a perilous journey indeed."

That seemed a tad overdramatic, considering I could hear the highway traffic from where we stood.

"From this day forward," Eli continued, "we offer no more guidance. It becomes your charge to thrive and survive. We only watch and judge." He took each of our hands and clasped them warmly. "Best wishes and strength." Then he turned to Angel and did the same before walking away.

"Well," said Angel, "I should get back to my folks so we can make our plans for the day." She picked up her bowl and waved her spoon. "Best wishes and strength!"

I turned to Mom. "We need a game plan."

Mom sat at the table. "All right. I suppose we knock out the most important items first."

I nodded. "Maslow's hierarchy of needs. On the most basic level, we need air, water, food, and sleep."

"Air . . ." Mom took a deep breath. "Check. Water from the pump . . . Check. Food . . ."

"Is very lacking," I said as my stomach gnawed at itself. "Let's start with that. We can't live off peaches alone. What other food sources do we have?"

We both glanced around the clearing where other families were strategizing their days. With this many people, there'd be a rush to find resources.

"Are you thinking what I'm thinking?" I asked Mom.

"That if we eat Dylan we can take care of two problems at once?" She smiled to let me know she was kidding. Or insane.

I leaned in and so did she. "There are cows and chickens in the barn and vegetables in the garden," I whispered. "But not enough for nine families."

Mom nodded and leaned back. "How about I take care of the meats, and you take care of the veggies."

I studied her closely. "By meats, you mean . . ."

She rolled her eyes. "Not your cousin."

"Okay," I said, starting to my feet. Mom grabbed my arm.

"Not so fast," she said under her breath. "Or everyone will know." She slowly stood and I copied her. "We're just going for a nice . . ."

Dylan sprinted past our table.

"Run!" cried Mom, heading for the barn.

I took off toward the garden, and judging by the shouts and pounding footfalls behind me, I wasn't alone. The corn was plentiful enough that I could save it for later. Instead I grabbed half a dozen squashes and handfuls of beans and turned to pluck out some carrots growing to one side.

Angel's entire family was in the garden, with both Angel and Aunt Zoe holding their dresses out in front while Uncle Deke tossed vegetables into them.

I created a makeshift basket with my own skirts and continued down the line, watching one of my distant aunts claw at the dirt around some leafy green stalks that turned out to be potato bunches.

I crouched carefully, keeping my vegetables in my dress, and dug my fingers into the earth, stopping every so often to tug on the stalk to see if it was loose. Sweat started to drip down my forehead, both from the effort and from knowing I was missing out on so many other vegetables as I watched people work around me.

Finally, I felt the roots start to give and jerked with all my might. About eight dirt-covered potatoes appeared on the end of the stalk. I let out a loud "Woohoo!" and tucked the bunch of potatoes under my skirt, where nobody could get at them. Then I scrabbled at the dirt for more.

"Need help?" Mom spoke over my shoulder, and I jumped.

"What are you doing here?" I asked. "You should be in the barn."

"I'm done there," she said, crouching beside me and scooping up dirt with our porridge spoon. "And you're almost out of available food here."

I straightened and looked around with wide eyes. Little scraps of vegetation littered the garden plot, the dark brown dirt from below the surface peppering the lighter soil on top. The plot was practically barren.

"Let's give it a pull," said Mom, dropping her spoon into a pocket. She and I both wrapped our hands around the stalk, ripping it from the ground . . . minus the potatoes.

"Shoot!" I shouted.

"I've got this," said Mom, nudging me. "Leave your vegetables here and go grab whatever else you can find."

I dropped all my gatherings beside her and scanned the garden again to see what would be worthwhile. A watermelon, free of its vine, rested in the middle of a random patch of dirt, no doubt dropped by someone in a hurry.

I hoisted up my skirt and ran for it, at the same moment that Angel approached from the other side. She might have had more energy from breakfast, but I was running lighter with nothing in my stomach. I reached it seconds before she did. Angel still grabbed for it and tried to yank it out of my arms.

"Let go!" I shouted. "I had it first."

"You can eat meat!" she shouted back. "Vegetables are all my family has."

And then she tried to bite my hand.

"Hey, you're supposed to be vegetarian!" I squawked, bouncing my hip against hers. Angel stumbled backward, thrown off balance, and I escaped with the watermelon tucked close to my chest. I sprinted back to Mom, who regarded me with wide eyes.

"What was that about?"

"Hippies . . . are . . . violent," I managed between breaths.

"Well, I can always fight her off with these," said Mom, holding up the second bunch of potatoes.

"Those are even bigger than the first ones!" I said, helping Mom to her feet.

"Load me up," she said, holding her dress out in front of her.

I piled in the vegetables, and we staggered under the weight of our haul back to the manor.

"So, how many eggs did you get?" I asked, climbing the stairs.

"None," said Mom.

I stopped on the landing and faced her. "None? Did you spend all your time getting milk?"

"No," said Mom, pushing me toward the door. "Keep walking. These potatoes aren't getting any lighter."

I did as she said but talked over my shoulder. "If you didn't get any eggs or milk, what did you get?"

"Something even better," she said, opening the door to our room.

A cow was tied to the bedpost.

I almost dropped the watermelon. "Wha—"

Something hammered and scratched from inside the footlocker.

Two chickens.

I gasped. "No."

"Ta-da!" said Mom.

I tugged her the rest of the way into the room and locked the door behind us.

"What did you do?" I hissed.

Mom blinked at me. "I . . . brought a cow and two chickens upstairs. I thought that was pretty obvious."

"*How* did nobody see you?" I asked.

She bit her lip. "I may have tried to bring in a goat first, and they were busy chasing it around the library."

I ran my fingers through my hair. "We sleep here, Mom."

"And now so do they," said Mom, petting the cow. It blinked slowly at her and butted its head against her side.

"I think I'll call you Queenie because you were a royal pain to get up the stairs." Mom turned to me and laughed. "The chickens were much easier. I just put KFC under one arm and Popeye—"

"Oh my god, I don't care!" I shouted. "We can't keep farm animals in our bedroom!"

Mom frowned. "Clearly, you don't see how clever I am. Everyone else grabbed eggs and milk. I grabbed the sources. Now we'll never run out . . . and we have entertainment for the evenings!"

I sighed and leaned against the door. "Can't we put them someplace else?"

Mom waved a dismissive hand. "You'll hardly notice they're here. Isn't that right?" She tugged on Queenie's halter.

Despite all the madness, at least our food situation was under control, even if it *did* take away from our last basic need: sleep.

The second most important needs were safety and security. We needed light, which came from candles, and we had maybe one more night's worth before ours were useless. To make the candles, I'd need lard for the wax and string for the wick. Unless I could steal some candles from the kitchen.

I tiptoed downstairs and started opening cupboards.

Not a scrap of food or conveniences. Just dishware, cookware, and buckets of lard.

Great-Aunt Muriel had wanted to make this hard on us.

I grabbed a bucket of lard and a small pot and spoon, carrying them all outside. Then, when I was sure nobody was looking, I snuck down to Caleb's craft shop in search of string for the wicking.

When I walked in, he was hammering a piece of metal into a disc but stopped and smiled.

"Sorry, hi!" I said with a wave. "I was looking for some string?"

"You don't have to be sorry," he said, putting down his hammer. "*I* should be, for letting Dylan crash our date." He froze. "Or . . . you know . . . not date. *Day*. Which was actually in the evening." He looked as if he wanted to jump into the forge.

"Our duh?" I stammered, wide-eyed. Then I cleared my throat and tried again. "Our date?"

"Was it not? Sorry, I guess—"

I took a step forward. "No, you were right! I mean . . . I wanted it to be." A blush warmed my cheeks.

Caleb's grin returned. "Good. Then . . . maybe we could try again tonight?"

I pretended to think on it. "I don't know. I already have a bracelet. What else would I need you for?"

"Earrings?"

I laughed and Caleb held up a hand. "You think I'm joking."

He rummaged in a drawer and pulled out a strip of leather punched with holes. From several dangled intricately shaped earrings.

"You made these?" I asked, unhooking one that had a trio of tinkling metal leaves.

"Well, the posts are surgical steel, but the rest is all me," he said. "And if you want, you can help me design a pair for you."

I put the earring down and faced him. "You spend a lot of time in here making stuff to sell, don't you?"

For some reason, Caleb bristled at that and went back to

his anvil. "I guess," he said, pushing on the bellows. The room got exponentially hotter as the flames grew.

"It's not a bad thing," I said, wincing from the heat. "It's just . . . I think you might be overdoing it. Kids our age only work this hard in sweatshops." I wiped my forehead and showed him my hand. "And this is getting pretty close."

Caleb smirked and picked up a pair of tongs. "Unfortunately, I don't have a choice. While you and your family have the luxury of competing for a fortune, my folks and I are just barely getting by." He grabbed the metal disc with the tongs and plunged it into the fire.

I frowned. "Caleb, this isn't a luxury for me," I told him. "If my mom and I don't win, we can't afford to keep our business open. If that happens, we lose her business *and* our house."

He paused in rotating the disc. One side began to warp. When he saw what was happening, he quickly withdrew it. "I'm sorry," he said without looking at me.

"It's okay," I said. "I shouldn't have said anything about how you live *your* life. I'm sorry."

But for some reason, he didn't seem comforted.

My heart sank. "Do you . . . do you still want to hang out tonight?"

Caleb looked at me and nodded firmly. "Just the two of us."

"Good. I'll wear my best bracelet and my least smelly dress," I said.

One corner of his mouth slowly crept up into a smile. "It's a date."

I left the craft hut with a smile and some string and found my bucket of lard exactly where I'd left it. Apparently, Dylan had no reason to sabotage it, which meant he probably didn't know what it could be used for. Score one for me.

I spooned the lard into the pot and almost threw up when a big chunk of fat revealed a putrid liquid layer underneath. Maybe Mom and I didn't need candles. Maybe we could just develop night vision, like owls, or scream at objects to find them, like bats. I raised one arm to cover my nose and finished spooning. Then I melted the lard over a fire for Pukestravaganza #2.

"What are you cooking?" Mom walked up, her voice muffled by one hand over her nose and mouth.

"I'm not cooking; I'm making candles." I took a step back and studied her, chicken feathers smattering her clothes and hair. "What happened to you?"

"Oh, I thought I could get the chickens to play Duck, Duck, Goose," she said. "I was wrong."

"Really?"

"No. They seemed a little cramped in the chest, so I decided to move them to the bathtub."

"The bathtub where we take our baths?" I asked, raising an eyebrow.

"Relax. They struggled so much, I never got the chance before they flew out the window." Mom peered into the pot. "That's melting nicely."

I stared at her. "Excuse me?"

"I said the fat—"

"I'm not talking about the fat!" I banged the spoon against the pot, and bits of lard flew everywhere. "What happened to the chickens?"

Mom took the spoon, no doubt worried I might weaponize it. "I told you. They flew out the window."

"Chickens can't fly!"

"They can if it's a short distance," said Mom. "Or if they're incredibly athletic."

I continued to stare at her.

"Unfortunately, neither of those was true in our case," she said with a sheepish shrug.

I sighed.

"But we'll eat well today!" she said with a reassuring smile.

"We could've eaten well for two weeks!" I told her. "You didn't scare the cow, too, did you? Because I know they can't fly at all."

While we talked, I started making the candles. Gripping the string in the middle with both hands, I dipped the rest of it into the lard pot and then lifted it out.

"And since I'm on a roll, I've got more bad news," said Mom. "Because it could be seen as an unfair advantage, we're no longer allowed to spend time outside the contest with the staff." She paused. "A.k.a. Caleb."

A.k.a. date night was canceled.

"That's fine," I lied, though I wanted to dunk Dylan's head in the lard. I had a feeling he was behind this.

"Sorry, hon." Mom squeezed me to her. "But there are plenty of boys back home." She put the spoon she was holding on the table. "I'm going to pluck and cook those chickens before flies eat the good parts."

She kissed the top of my head, and I went back to dipping candles, quietly seething inside.

Until I saw Caleb.

He came out of his craft hut and made a direct line for me, clutching a small white box in one hand.

"Those candles are looking pretty good!" he said.

"Yeah, but they're not smelling pretty good," I said. "What's that you've got?" I nodded to the box.

He grinned and ducked his head. "Just a little something for you. Sorry I got so defensive earlier."

I took it from him and opened it. Inside were the leaf earrings I'd been admiring. I beamed up at him. "These are awesome! Thank you so much!"

"I thought you'd like to have those, even though we're going to make you some special ones tonight," he said.

"Tonight," I repeated, remembering Mom's warning.

"We *are* still on for tonight, right?" asked Caleb.

It took me roughly two seconds of hesitation before I answered.

"Yes, of course I'll be there."

Chapter Eight

Y ou want me to what?" asked Angel. "You can't be serious."

I clasped my hands in front of me. "Just for tonight. I already promised Caleb I'd meet him before I knew the contest rules."

Angel crossed her arms over her chest. "You know you could get disqualified. You really want to do that for a guy who lives hundreds of miles away?"

"Nobody's going to find out," I said. "And Caleb isn't going to say anything. Please just cover for me for, like, an hour."

Angel studied me closely. "One hour. Sixty minutes."

"Sixty minutes," I promised.

She sighed and waved me away. "Go. Have fun. Fall in love."

"Thank you!" I squealed, and hugged her.

"Oh! Ack!" she cried, pushing me away. "I'm pretty sure he's not going to fall in love with that smell. What have you been doing?"

I shrank back. "Picking vegetables in the hot, hot sun, and boiling rancid fat. You wouldn't happen to have any all-natural body-odor remedies, would you?"

"Vinegar and mint," said Angel. "Mint to mask the smell, and vinegar to prevent more. I actually have a solution that combines both."

She disappeared into her bathroom and returned a moment later with a small bottle. I tried to take it from her, but she pulled her hand back.

"I'm doing you three favors," she said. "I want something in return."

"Three favors?" I repeated.

"This stuff can be used as a deodorizer *and* mouthwash," she said. "And I'm lying to your mother for you."

I nodded. "Fine. What do you want?"

"Oh, I think you know."

I ground my teeth together but nodded again. "I'll be right back."

Slipping into my bedroom, I shuffled through the feathers

on the floor and got on my hands and knees. We'd chosen to stash all our fruits and vegetables under the bed, so I rolled the watermelon out and hefted it into my arms. Queenie mooed from her corner by the wardrobe.

"Don't tell Mom," I said, closing the door behind me.

"Pleasure doing business with you," said Angel when I presented her with the melon. She handed over the bottle. "And good luck in the afternoon challenge."

"Yeah," I said, pocketing it. "You too."

But I knew neither of us really meant it.

After a delicious lunch of second-story chicken, Mom and I joined the other families in a field where targets had been set up fifty yards away. Eli leaned against a post jutting from the ground, one of about twenty posts scattered at random around us.

"It would appear that some of you lack in foodstuffs," he said. "In colonial times, this was when it became necessary to find more. Therefore, we give you the opportunity to go 'hunting.'" He crooked his fingers.

"Did air quotes exist in colonial times?" Mom asked me in a low voice. I shushed her.

"It would be truer to have you shoot and kill your own animals," he said, causing Angel's whole family to gasp. "But I do not feel as if you can all be trusted with weaponry." I might have imagined it, but I was pretty sure his eyes flicked to Dylan.

"Therefore, using bow and arrow, you will attempt to hit the target, the bull's-eye specifically. The closest two will win a basket of foodstuffs."

"Easy," said Mom. "I took archery at summer camp."

Several other people murmured confidence in themselves.

"Let's get shooting," said Dylan, rubbing his hands together. "Where's the gear?"

Eli smiled and indicated a stack of bows propped against a tree. "I've provided the bows. You must provide the arrows."

"How's that?" someone asked.

"We have to make them," I said.

"Correct!" said Eli. "All you should require are sticks and feathers." When he mentioned the first item, he pointed to the trees, and when he mentioned the second . . . Caleb rolled up in a wagon with another guy about his age in a hat that said TOM'S TURKEYS.

"Uh-oh," said Angel.

Both guys jumped down and grabbed a roll of baling wire off the back. In five minutes' time, they'd unrolled it all around the posts I'd noticed, and soon the families were enclosed in a large patch of field.

And then . . . the demons were unleashed.

A dozen turkeys who clearly did not want to lose their feathers sprinted from their cage to the far end of the enclosure.

"You have until the sand runs out to prepare three arrows per family," said Eli. He held up a large hourglass and flipped it over.

Everyone burst into action, running straight for the turkeys. Mom grabbed my arm and held me back.

"Everyone else is gonna get their feathers first!" I said, trying to pull free.

"No," said Mom, crouching low. "They're going to drive the turkeys right to us."

Sure enough, half the birds were headed back toward our side of the enclosure.

"There." She pointed. "The one that looks like it has a perm."

We both dove for the same bird, which squawked and let out a Gobble of Doom.

Mom held it tight. "Get four feathers!"

I winced and said, "Sorry, Mr. Turkey." Then I grabbed the feathers and yanked. The second they were in my hand, Mom released the bird and grabbed my free hand.

"Let's go!"

She pulled me out of the enclosure, and I was happy to see we were the first ones free.

"Grab the straightest, longest sticks you can find," she instructed me. "I'll split the feathers."

I scanned the ground for fallen branches, picking some up and throwing others aside. After I found the best, I glanced at the hourglass in Eli's hand. It was halfway empty. I glanced into the turkey pen. One of the families was still inside.

"Tori!" Mom called to me.

I hurried over with the branches and she studied them, throwing away all but three.

"Good job," she said. Mom took a knife out of her pocket and sharpened one end of each stick into a point. "Now we add feathers."

"With what?" I asked. "Glue?"

She sawed three grooves along the sides of the opposite end, sliding the vein of a halved feather into each groove.

"Cool!" I said, admiring her handiwork when she finished the first one. "Where did you learn that?"

Mom smirked. "I'm a dressmaker, sweetheart. My job is making pieces fit seamlessly."

She finished the second arrow, then the third, and cut a notch in the feathered end of each for the bowstring.

"Shall we test them out?" she asked.

But before she'd even nocked the first arrow, Eli hollered for everyone to stop.

"Time has run out!" he cried. "Grab your bows and arrows and follow me to the targets." He pointed to the family still in the turkey enclosure. "Except you. Your time has run out for the contest as well."

The rest of us fell into step behind Eli, and while we walked, I stared at other people's arrows. They all looked pretty crude, with Angel's family's looking crudest of all.

Theirs didn't have feathers; they had leaves.

"Um . . ." I pointed at Angel's arrow.

"We couldn't do it," she said.

"How would you like it if someone chased you around the yard and pulled out your hair?" asked Aunt Zoe.

I fought the urge to roll my eyes. "You don't think those leaves are going to crumble under the pressure?"

"It was either this or get disqualified," said Uncle Deke.

"Enough idle chatter," said Eli. "You will surely startle your prey." He gestured to some hay bales with bull's-eyes painted on them.

Dylan snickered.

"Assemble a line and take your shots. The order matters not," said Eli, ignoring him.

And even though Mom and I were last in line, we placed first. Angel's family came in dead last.

"Congratulations," Aunt Zoe told us as Mom shifted the

weight of the food basket Eli had just handed her.

"Thanks," we both said.

"Do you want help carrying that?" I asked Mom. We were walking back to the manor. "It looks heavy."

"I think I can manage," she said. "You weighed a little more as a baby, and I carried you just fine."

"Gee, thanks," I said drily. But I couldn't be upset with our recent success. Just when I'd been starting to lose hope, Mom and I pulled it off.

"I don't think anyone expected us to do so well," I told her. "Not even me."

"Never doubt your mother," said Mom. "Who was the one who told you butter could get you unstuck from the heating duct?"

"Who was the one who got me stuck there in the first place?" I countered.

"Was it not the perfect hiding space for hide-and-seek?"

I was silent for a moment. "It was."

Mom grinned and bumped me with her shoulder. "So what do you say we eat dinner and then play a game I invented?" She held up a finger. "I promise it's not Yarn."

I smiled. "Actually, I have plans with Angel tonight. We're going to do something with that watermelon."

Mom nodded. "Okay, that sounds like fun."

After dinner, I snuck into the bathroom and slathered the vinegar and mint under my arms, even rubbing some into the fabric of my dress. I said good-bye to Mom and sprinted down the hall before she could see that I wasn't stopping at Angel's room.

Once I was sure the coast was clear, I crept from shadow to shadow down to the craft hut. Caleb opened the door before I even knocked. And he didn't look happy to see me.

"What's wrong?" I asked.

"My dad said it's against the rules for any of the contestants to hang out with us." He frowned and dropped his shoulders.

"I know," I said. "But . . . I still want to."

He perked up a bit. "Really? With me?"

"Well . . . yeah," I said, smiling. "But I'll leave if it'll get you in trouble."

Caleb took a step closer. "I won't say anything if you won't." He glanced around and gestured for me to come in.

I slipped through the doorway, feeling equal parts guilty and excited.

We didn't talk any about his family's financial situation or mine. Instead, he told me about his regular life outside the 1600s, and I told him about life in my town. We quizzed

each other on interests and likes and dislikes and teased each
other about them.

"You don't like hummus?" I asked.

"I don't like the texture," he said. "It's like eating that
white paste from kindergarten."

"You don't like the white paste from kindergarten?!"

Caleb laughed and placed a sheet of paper on the table
beside us. "Tell me what kind of earrings you want."

"Ones that will give me superpowers."

"Cute." He tapped me on the nose with his pencil. "But
something more realistic."

I thought a moment. "Can we make flower earrings?"

Caleb began sketching. "How many petals? Round or
pointed?"

"Five round ones." I watched while he drew. "Perfect."

Caleb picked up a piece of sheet metal and got to work on
the real thing. I wanted to stay and watch the whole process,
but the hour passed quicker than I expected and I had to say
good-bye.

"Sorry, but my cousin will only cover for me for so long."

"Your cousin knows you're here?" he asked, wide-eyed.

"Angel," I told him. "And don't worry, she'll keep it a
secret."

Caleb nodded. "I should have these done for you by tomorrow, but I don't know how I can get them to you." He ran a hand over his hair. "Unless you want to hang out again?"

My stomach did a flip-flop. "Sure!" I blurted. "I mean . . . whatever, yeah."

"Way to play it cool," Caleb said with a smile.

I laughed and we hugged good-bye, me praying the whole time that he wouldn't smell me and change his mind.

Before I left, he stepped outside and checked for signs of life. Then he turned and beckoned me forward. With one last wave, I darted from shadow to shadow again, all the way to the back door.

Which was locked.

"Shoot!" I whispered.

There was no doubt in my mind who did it, but at the moment I had more important things to worry about . . . like getting back inside. I prowled the length of windows until I found the one for Angel's room. Then I picked up a rock and threw it. It clicked loud against the glass and I ducked into the bushes. No movement from above.

I picked up another rock and threw it, pressing my back against the building. The curtains over Angel's window rustled.

I jumped out and started waving my arms but froze.

Mom was looking down at me.

She drew open the window and leaned out. "Tori? Well . . .

what on earth are you doing out there?" The confusion in her voice dripped with sarcasm. "I thought for *sure* you'd be here in Angel's room. Isn't that the strangest thing?"

And that's when I realized Dylan hadn't locked me out. Mom had.

"Please please please let me in!" I whispered as loud as I dared.

"Gee." Mom scratched her head. "I really wish I could, but since I'm not smart enough to figure out your plan, I'm probably not smart enough to unlock a door either." She shrugged. "Sorry! Have fun sleeping in the barn!"

And with that, she closed the window and shut the curtains.

As I sulked down the path to the barn and tried to find a patch of ground not covered in poop, I realized I didn't feel one bit guilty for what I did. If anything, Mom had brought it on herself for screwing up challenges and being a screwup in general.

Nope, I decided, settling down against a hay bale. *She* was the problem, not me.

Chapter Nine

$\mathcal{A}$ngel didn't share my opinion. We talked over breakfast, since I was in no mood to eat with Mom. Two cows had licked me during the night.

"Honestly, I can't blame her," said Angel. "I would never trick my parents like that."

I gawked at her as if she'd just declared hot dogs wholesome.

"You trick your parents every day!" I exclaimed. "Pretending to embrace their lifestyle and then borrowing perfume from me!"

"That's not the same," she said, scooping up porridge.

"How is it not?"

"It's not because it's not," replied Angel.

"Strong argument."

Angel put down her spoon. "Look. You and your mom have a bond most people would kill for. And when you lie to her, you break that bond and become just like . . ." She pointed to Dylan and his dad.

I scowled. "I am nothing like Dylan. You take that back."

"Okay, okay. But you still shouldn't trick your mom. You guys are supposed to be a team in this thing."

Angel was right. Mom and I needed to work like a team, and that meant apologizing, even if it was the last thing I wanted to do. Gritting my teeth, I approached the table where Mom was sitting with Aunt Zoe and Uncle Deke.

"Morning, honey!" chirped Mom. "Sleep well?"

"Two cows licked me," I told her.

Aunt Zoe and Uncle Deke exchanged mystified looks.

"Well, that's just because you're so sweet," said Mom with a sunny smile. "Did you need something?"

"I wanted to . . . apologize," I said through clenched teeth.

Mom cocked her head to one side. "That doesn't sound very genuine. Are you lying . . . again?"

Aunt Zoe cleared her throat at Uncle Deke, and the two of them got up from the table.

"No, I'm not lying," I said.

Mom leaned closer. "Are you lying about not lying?"

"No."

Mom leaned back. "Are you lying about not lying about not lying?"

"No!" I said, but a laugh escaped. It was hard to stay mad at my mom. "Okay, I really am sorry I upset you."

"That's better." She smiled and held her arms open. I sat down next to her and let her squish me. "Who's my favorite girl?"

I rolled my eyes. "Me."

"Who's your favorite mom?"

"You are."

"Darn right. And never forget it."

But an hour later, when the morning challenge came, I kind of did. Each family had to build a chair. A simple chair. Four legs, a seat, and a back.

Instead, Mom and I built the lovechild of stilts and a bookshelf.

"Did they have giraffes in America during colonial times?" I asked as we stood back to inspect our handiwork. "Because I feel that's the only creature who would benefit from this monstrosity."

"It's not *that* tall," said Mom, reaching up to pat one of the seats.

I frowned. "And how did we end up with that seat . . . and then another two feet above it?"

"I think one of the seats was supposed to be the back," said Mom. "But that's okay! The extra seat underneath just means you and a friend can both enjoy."

"None of my friends are two feet tall," I said.

"People were a lot shorter in colonial times," Mom said solemnly.

I shook my head and looked at the other teams' chairs. And then I looked at ours again. "We should've followed the instructions better," I said. "Why did you say you knew what you were doing?"

Mom sighed and ran her fingers through her hair. "I don't know, Tori. I built your crib without any instructions."

"It was a nylon pop-up crib," I told her. "All you had to do was unfold it. This"—I patted our so-called chair—"was a little more complicated. We should've followed the instructions."

"I heard you the first time," said Mom, sounding a little testy. "What do you want me to do?"

"Take things more seriously!" I said. "I want to win!"

Eli started making the rounds and declared the family with the baby as winners. We, of course, came in last.

"Though there is one overall winner, you are all winners

since you now have a creation of your own to take with you."

"Or use as firewood to burn designer dresses that *somebody* can't make money selling," said Dylan, laughing at me and Mom.

That was a low blow.

"Dylan . . . " said his dad in a warning tone.

"Why do you even pretend to threaten him?" I exploded. "We both know you're going to give Dylan whatever he wants."

Furious, I turned to Dylan. "Wah wah! Counting all my allowance money takes *so* long."

They both just stared at me, speechless.

Mom was on me in a flash, fingers gripping my arm so tight that if I tried to leave, I'd have been doing it minus a limb.

"Victoria," she said in a soft voice, "apologize now."

"Sorry," I said without an ounce of feeling.

Mom's face darkened, and she dragged me tripping and stumbling away from the others, including Caleb who was cleaning up after the chair building.

"*What* has gotten into you?" Mom asked, letting me go.

"Gee, I guess I woke up on the wrong side of the bed." I snapped my fingers. "Oh, no—wait. I *didn't*."

I twisted on my heel and left.

"Where are you going?" Mom called after me.

I pointed at the barn. "To my room!"

Mom was smart enough not to follow, and the cows inside were smart enough to stay out of my way. I kicked a bucket and sent it flying across the barn before I plopped down on the ground and quietly seethed. And then I fell asleep.

Someone shook my shoulder, and I woke up swinging.

"It's me! It's me!" said Caleb, holding up his hands.

I struggled to a sitting position and ran my fingers through my snarled hair. "What . . . what are you doing here?"

"I saw you get a little upset earlier," he said. "I just wanted to see if you're okay."

"Well, thanks," I said. "But . . . I probably won't be until this contest is over."

"That bad, huh?" Caleb settled on the ground next to me.

"My mom is normally great," I said. "But she doesn't seem to get how much is riding on this contest. And that what she does affects *both* of us." I shrugged. "But I probably shouldn't have taken it out on Uncle Max. I'm sure he already knows how bad Dylan is without me telling him."

Caleb grew quiet. "I'm sorry you got in trouble for seeing me."

I shrugged. "It wasn't so bad."

"Tori, you slept in the barn." He gestured around us. "I don't want that to happen again."

I knew the right response. I knew what I should have said. I knew I should have ended things right then.

But . . .

"Maybe we could meet during the day instead," I said.

This experience was a major suckfest. I should at least get *some* happiness out of it.

"Yeah?" said Caleb with a hopeful smile. "You won't get caught?"

"Not if my mom thinks I'm doing chores for the contest," I said. "I'll tell her I'm gathering wood, and then I'll just happen to run into you in the forest."

Caleb's eyes sparkled mischievously. "I like that. We can have a secret code. Like, you'll tell your mom a task, and I'll meet you at that location."

I smiled and got to my feet, spirits lifted. "I might just make it after all," I said.

And it was exactly how I got through the next few days. Every day, Mom and I would tank one of the contests, and every day, instead of yelling at Mom, I'd announce that I was off to pick peaches or try to catch fish. Caleb and I would hang out for a couple of hours while I did those things, and then I'd head back to Mom.

Strangely, for every challenge we lost, we'd excel at a different one. We were terrible when it came to chopping wood but number one at making candles (thanks to my personal efforts). We didn't know a thing about healing herbs, but Mom could ride circles on horseback around everyone else.

By the end of the first week, Mom and I were in third behind Angel's family and Dylan and Uncle Max, and the number of competing families was down to six.

But then . . . Saturday came.

We all, admittedly, smelled pretty ripe by this point, even with a change of clothing and me rubbing minty vinegar under my arms. I was surprised Caleb didn't maintain a safe distance or force me to stay downwind whenever we were together. So it came as a relief on Saturday morning when our challenge was . . . doing laundry.

"I thought you could all use a break," said Eli, "and a reduction in odor."

We all laughed and headed down to the river on the edge of the property. Since I was always the one who did the laundry at home, I took it upon myself to gather our dirty clothes, except the ones we were wearing. Those we'd wash once the others were clean.

"So, how are you handling not getting to see Caleb?" asked Mom, dunking one of her shifts in the river.

"Who?" I asked in my most nonchalant voice. "Oh, Eli's son?"

Mom rolled her eyes. "Yes, I'm sure he's *that* difficult for you to remember. I thought you'd be pining away for him every night, but instead you play Guess Who Died Here? with me."

"That's not true," I said. "Tuesday I played Remember the Mall? with Angel."

We both looked at my cousin, who was helping her mom knock dust out of a blanket with sticks. Although Angel was using so much force, it was like she thought the blanket was a piñata full of makeup samples.

"How she's survived so long without her smartphone is beyond me," mumbled Mom.

"You know what I wonder . . . how Uncle Max and Dylan have survived so long," I said, glancing downriver.

"What do you mean? They're good competitors."

"Yeah, but they never win any food and I never see them looking, and I *know* Dylan didn't get very much when we did the mad scramble."

Mom shrugged, still watching Zoe and Angel. "I'm sure they have their ways."

I nodded at my cousin. "You think we should give our blanket a beating?"

"Or we could let Queenie stomp on it."

"That is the laziest idea you've ever come up with," I said. "Even lazier than keeping refrigerators in our bedrooms at home and cereal under the beds."

"Think of the time savings!" said Mom. "Not to mention the luxury of always having breakfast in bed." She finished cleaning her shift and tossed it in the basket. "Someday you'll come to your senses and realize what a genius I am. Look how well having Queenie upstairs has worked."

"Oh, yeah," I said, flashing her a sarcastic thumbs-up. "That milk every morning makes the poop in my slippers worth it."

We finished our washing and then turned to lathering the clothes we were wearing . . . while we were still in them.

"Okay, I was wrong. *This* is the laziest idea you've ever had," I said, dropping down into the water to rinse myself off.

"You know, I really think we could take this whole contest," said Mom. "Especially if we keep winning challenges."

"Exactly," I said. "*If* we keep winning challenges. We can't let Dylan and his dad have any more. Or Angel and her folks. We have to take this seriously."

"Who says I'm not?" Mom disappeared under the water and emerged a moment later. "Geez, this dress is heavy."

Mom stepped out of the water and pulled the gown off over her head so that she was only wearing her shift.

"Mom!" I covered my face with my hands. "Please, please put on some clothes or burst into flame . . . something to distract from the fact that you're standing around in your underwear."

"What? We're all family," said Mom. "And besides, it's

full-length underwear. Hey, how many points do I get for this basket?" She balled up her dress and spun around, launching it toward our container of clean clothes.

She missed by a mile, and it ended up in a tree.

"There go our hopes of you being drafted by the WNBA," I said, clambering up the riverbank to retrieve it.

Mom had thrown the dress with enough force to lodge it in some branches. I did my best to extract the fabric without tearing it, and in the process I saw something that didn't normally belong in a tree.

A video camera.

It was a black orb no bigger than my hand, wedged into a nook and duct taped in place. Whoever had left it there did it intentionally.

I dropped the dress and grabbed the video camera.

"Hey, Mom, come over here!" I called.

"Really, you just throw my clothes on the ground?" she asked, kicking the dress to one side. "What have you got?"

I held it out to her. "I found it in this tree. Looks like Eli's been filming the family."

Mom frowned. "What? Why?"

"TV stations are always looking for new reality shows, right?"

"Nooo. He wouldn't." Mom glanced over her shoulder. "Would he?"

"Only one way to find out," I said, taking the video camera back from her. "Hey, Eli!"

I charged down the hill, toward the river.

Mom chased after me. "Honey, wait! That might not be a good idea!"

"Eli!" I called again.

Everyone, including Eli, looked over. I stopped in front of him, waving the black orb.

"Found your video camera," I said, tossing it to him.

Eli looked startled when he caught it. "My what?"

People gathered around to look at it. Eli furrowed his brow and inspected it. "What is this? Where did you get this?"

"Oh, like you don't know," I said.

He glanced up, nothing in his eyes but confusion.

"Oh," I said. "You *don't* know. It's a video camera," I explained. "I thought it was yours, but"—I studied his outfit and reflected on the past week—"now that I'm thinking about it, you're not really the type of person who would care about filming something for reality TV." I cringed. "Sorry."

Beside me, I could see Mom cover her eyes and shake her head.

"Then whose camera is this?" I wondered aloud.

There was a buzz of conversation from everyone gathered as we all began to speculate.

The confusion in Eli's eyes changed to something else—realization. Then they fixed on me. And they were not friendly.

"This object you accuse me of owning." He held up the video camera. "You name it as if you know it."

"It's not mine, if that's what you're getting at," I said.

"Yet you know what it is and you know what it does," he said.

I marveled at him. "Yeah. It's a video camera. Everybody knows what they do."

Eli shrugged and I continued.

"It takes moving images of people?" I held my arms open. "Seriously?"

"Careful." Mom spoke out of the side of her mouth. "It's a trap."

He inspected it closer. "It has a maker's year imprinted upon it. 2015." He looked up at me. "Yet this is the seventeenth century."

I sighed and stared at the sky. *"Shoot."*

"You have come into possession of an item from centuries hence, armed with knowledge of its function," said Eli. "Spend some time with your family today, Miss Porter. Tomorrow you will stand trial."

"Trial?" Mom and I said in unison.

Eli nodded to her. "Aye. Your daughter . . . she be a witch."

Chapter Ten

I blinked at Eli, since my eyes were the only muscle group in my body not frozen in shock.

"Sorry," I said, tapping my ear, "but I think river water's sloshing around in my head. It sounded like you said . . . I'm a witch?"

Eli nodded solemnly. "Aye. You bring me a witch's ball that can capture people inside—"

"I didn't say . . ." I broke off, realizing that any explanation would work against me.

"This is an item of magic. You are in possession of said magic. Therefore, you must be a witch!"

I goggled at him. "I told you, I found it! It isn't mine!"

"Perhaps it were the Devil who led you to it," he said with a shrug. "And you know who works with the Devil? A witch!" He pointed at me.

"This is ridiculous," said Mom, wrapping an arm around me. "Shouldn't you be focusing your attention on finding the owner of the video camera?"

The next words out of Eli's mouth completely jarred me. In a thick Boston accent, he said, "Look, lady, regardless of who it belongs to, your daughter's either in the game or she's not. If she's in, she has to suffer the consequences." He held his arms out, as if awaiting our decision.

I separated myself from Mom and stepped forward. "I'm still in the game. What are the consequences?"

"You've been found a witch," said Eli, resuming his colonial voice. "You must stand trial and account for your actions. And so must your mother."

It was Mom's turn to drop her jaw. "Me? What did I do?"

Felicity spoke up. "You defended a witch. Only a fellow witch would decry her." She glanced around at the rest of the family members, as if encouraging them to speak out of turn.

Nobody said a word. And several people took a few steps away from us.

"Thanks for the support," I muttered. "I can promise I'm

not a witch. I don't have any warts, cats, or flying broomsticks."

"Reserve your arguments for the trial," said Eli. "And enjoy your last night of freedom."

He climbed the slope up to the manor, and everyone followed. I turned to Mom, who gave me a strained smile.

"I hate to say I told you so," she said.

I shook my head. "Don't you get it? If we're accused of witchcraft, they won't let us stay in the competition."

Mom shrugged. "So what? At least we had fun. And if you remember your promise to me, you were going to enjoy this experience and *not* worry about money?"

I gripped her arms. "But, Mom, we're *so* close to winning . . . to our troubles being a thing of the past. All we need is a few lucky breaks, but this isn't one of them!"

I plopped down on the grass. Everything always seemed to be against us. Me and Mom versus the world. Maybe if my dad were still around, he'd know what to do.

"Come on." Mom grabbed me under the armpits and lifted. "On your feet. We won't be disqualified. I'll come up with something."

I let her help me up. "I just hope it works," I said with a sigh, and trudged up the hill. Mom let me walk alone.

Halfway to the manor, I met Caleb running down.

"I heard what happened. Are you okay?" he asked.

"Your dad accused me of witchcraft," I said. "And now I'm standing in front of you in a soggy old dress. I've had better days."

Caleb covered his eyes with a hand. "I'm not even looking."

I smiled. "You know, I'm pretty sure that if you're not supposed to be talking to me as a contestant, you definitely shouldn't be talking to me as a witch."

"I can just say I came to tell you the time of your trial. It's right after breakfast, by the way," said Caleb, "but unfortunately, tomorrow I'll have to be on the side that's convinced you're a witch." He made a face. "Sorry."

"It's okay," I said. "At least I'll get one last bowl of gruel."

We walked in silence for a moment, and I noticed that his steps kept bringing him closer and closer to me.

"Can I give you some advice?" he asked. "My dad has nothing against you personally, but I can tell he's really excited for this witch trial. The odds aren't in your favor."

I frowned. "How very *Hunger Games*."

"Come up with a pretend backstory for yourself," said Caleb. "If you talk about modern times, it'll just confirm you're a witch. Play along, and you might get away with just a warning."

I paused and took his arm so that he was forced to look at me. "And if I don't—"

He shook his head. "You can't think that way."

"But if I don't," I pressed, "my mom and I will have to go home. And home is very far away."

Caleb stared at the ground. "I know."

I wanted to hug him, but we were out in the open where anyone could see, and a hug probably wasn't something you gave a contestant who was on trial for witchcraft. My fingers squeezed his arm instead.

I let my hand drop down by his, and our fingers touched for a fraction of a second before he pulled his away.

Caleb sighed. "Good luck tomorrow. And remember, play the game."

"Thanks," I told him, and we parted ways by the back door.

When I got up to the room, Mom was talking to Queenie.

"They don't burn people at the stake anymore, do they?"

I cleared my throat. "I think the smell of burning hair discourages them."

Mom smirked at me. "They could shave our heads first, you know."

I flopped down on the bed. "Maybe we should create backstories for ourselves. Really get into character for the trial."

Mom laughed. "You want us to . . . " She paused and then stared out the window. "Maybe that would work."

"So, I was thinking I could be me but add a few details about what a good person I am."

"Not too many details," said Mom, chewing a fingernail. "You want it to be believable."

Even deep in thought, Mom could insult me.

"And you could be—"

Mom held up a hand. "I have something in mind. Just let me think it through."

She pulled a chair in front of the window and sat. I watched her for a few minutes and then got up to visit Angel. When I knocked on her bedroom door, however, she barely opened it a crack.

"Listen, Tori, I love you like a cousin—"

"We *are* cousins," I interrupted.

"But I can't be associated with you right now. Not when my family is so close to taking this contest. If people think *we're* witches too . . ."

She let the thought trail, and I frowned.

"Seriously? You're afraid of catching my witchcraft cooties?"

"I knew you'd understand! Love you, bye!" she said, closing the door in my face.

I didn't even bother knocking on Aunt Zoe and Uncle Deke's door. I had a feeling I'd get the same response. I went back to our bedroom, where Mom was still sitting in the chair, staring out the window.

"A watched sun never sets," I told her. "Which would actually work well for us, since the trial's tomorrow after breakfast."

Mom just nodded, so I let her be. When it was time for bed, she was finally willing to get up from the chair, but she was still too deep in thought.

"Tomorrow morning," she said, "I don't want you to disagree with anything I say."

I propped myself on my elbows. "Why? What are you going to say?"

Mom shook her head. "Just trust me. I have a plan."

The next morning, after a breakfast neither of us could eat, we were led to the clearing behind the manor, where rows of benches had been set facing a table with two chairs. Mom and I knew our place and took our seats.

"These chairs came out much nicer than ours," she said, wiggling her butt in her seat. "I wonder if we can take them when we leave. As souvenirs."

" 'Sorry you turned out to be witches, but here's some lovely furniture'?" I asked. "Please take this seriously."

"I am," said Mom. "But it was giving me forehead wrinkles, so I had to lighten up a bit." She put a hand on my arm. "Don't worry. Everything is going to work out."

The back door creaked open, and the rest of the families came out to fill the seats.

"I hope you're right," I said. "Because here come our judge, jury, and executioners."

Eli, Felicity, and Caleb marched over from their quarters, and Eli's eyes shone with excitement. He really *was* going to enjoy this. After a brief introduction, Eli asked Mom and me to introduce ourselves. With a deep breath, I launched into my story.

"My name is Victoria Porter," I said. "I'm the daughter of a seamstress and a soldier. I take care of wounded animals in the woods—"

Eli was staring at his fingernails, completely ignoring me. I caught Caleb's eye, and he shrugged.

So much for playing the game.

"And I'm lead singer for a band named Plymouth Rock," I finished.

Eli strolled in front of our table. "Are you a witch?"

"Nope," I said, getting up. "That was easy!"

"Sit down," said Eli. "We are not finished."

"Oh." I sat.

Mom leaned over. "You didn't read up on the Salem witch trials?"

Eli slammed his fists on the table between Mom and me, and we jumped back, startled.

"Conspiring as witches do?" he asked.

"Actually, she was complimenting your beard," I said. "It's quite fluffy. Do you volumize?"

Eli narrowed his eyes. "You speak in words well beyond your years. As a witch would."

"As a well-educated girl would," I corrected.

"And your tongue is barbed," he said with a frown. "You show little respect to your elders."

"Only the ones who deserve it," I retorted.

"She didn't show my dad any respect!" Dylan called from his bench. "Burn her at the stake!"

I tugged on Eli's sleeve and pointed at Dylan. "If I was really a witch? He'd be a smoldering pile of ashes right now."

Several people gasped.

"Exactly what a witch would say!" whispered Felicity.

I rolled my eyes.

"Exactly what a witch would do!" she whispered.

I sighed and leaned back. "So you think I'm a witch because I found a camera and roll my eyes?"

"And levitate!" someone called from the back.

"Who . . . " I craned my neck to see. A random half-cousin I didn't even know that well. But she and her family were in fourth place, right behind Mom and me.

"You saw me levitate?" I repeated. "Where's the proof?"

"I saw Tori levitate too," said Dylan.

I scowled at him. "I saw you turn into a pig. Why aren't *you* on the stand?"

"Silence, witch!" said Eli. He turned to my mother. "What say you?"

Mom folded her hands in front of her and leaned forward. "I say . . . that I am your long-lost sister." She glanced at Eli's wife. "Hey, sis!"

Eli blinked in confusion. "What?"

"I am your long-lost sister, and Tori is your long-lost niece." She gestured to me. "You and your wife planted us in the contest to steal the old bird's fortune. But yesterday I told you we would no longer help you perform such a vile deed, and you retaliated by accusing us of witchcraft."

"This . . . this is preposterous!" blustered Eli. He faced his wife, who did not look pleased.

"Why do you think we've been winning challenges?" Mom asked the audience. "Because my brother"—she winked at Eli—"helps us. But he can't let us win all the time, so that's why we occasionally do so bad."

The family members began whispering among themselves.

"Do you think it's true?"

"They *are* pretty incompetent."

I couldn't help feeling mildly insulted.

"This is not about me, it is about you!" Eli pointed at Mom

and me. "Your daughter is a witch! She knows of magic!"

"Because *you* taught her, remember?" said Mom. She looked out at the crowd and rolled her eyes, laughing. "So forgetful."

Eli's face was now the color of a sliced watermelon. "We are not related!"

Mom spread her arms open. "Prove it. My accusations are as valid as yours."

"I . . . you . . . she!" Eli grabbed at his hair.

Mom leaned forward and whispered, "Nobody here knows my side of the family, so my words have weight. Unless you want to mention DNA testing, which didn't exist in colonial times and would make *you* look like a witch, drop the accusation or everyone will think you're cheating and mass chaos will ensue."

The clearing was completely quiet, as if even the birds were waiting for an answer.

"I may . . . have jumped to conclusions," Eli said begrudgingly. "It is possible that these two strangers are simple humans."

"Very simple!" called Dylan.

"Are you looking in a mirror?" I asked.

Mom nudged me into silence. "Then it is possible we are not actually related," she said.

"This trial is over," said Eli, shoulders slumping, "and all witchcraft charges are dropped."

Everyone on the benches applauded.

Now they were supportive.

"Please follow me to the barn for the morning challenge," he said in a dull tone.

Before I could do that, I had to turn to Mom and throw my arms around her.

"That was brilliant!" I said.

"The best defense is a good offense," said Mom, hugging me back. "I told you I'd come up with something."

Angel approached the table with her parents.

"Looks like you live to fight another day!" she said, hugging me.

"Congratulations," added Aunt Zoe. "I'm not sure if that's the smartest move I've seen or the most foolish."

Mom and I looked at one another and then at Aunt Zoe.

"What do you mean?"

"I have a feeling you're going to start finding this contest a lot more difficult," said Aunt Zoe.

"You personally insulted Eli and his family," said Uncle Deke. "He's not going to forget that. Neither will they."

I swallowed hard.

Caleb.

Chapter Eleven

"You want cheese omelets?" Mom asked the next morning.

"Huh?" I turned away from our bedroom window. I'd been sitting in the window seat since sunrise, watching Caleb's craft hut.

Mom gave me a sympathetic smile. "He still hasn't seen your note?"

I shook my head. "I tried to talk to him after the trial, then after the first challenge, then after the *second* challenge. He keeps avoiding me."

"I can't believe he's so upset," said Mom. "It was all in good fun."

I buried my head in my hands. "Mom, you implied he and his family were a bunch of cheaters. Even if it wasn't true, you still made them look bad."

"Well, he needs to get over it, and *you* need to get over *him*," she said. "Now *do* you want a cheese omelet?"

I poked my head through the neck hole of my dress. "Kraft singles haven't even been invented yet. Where are you going to get cheese?"

"I made a batch," Mom said.

"Milk you accidentally left on a sunny windowsill isn't cheese," I informed her.

"Ha ha ha," she said, pulling her hair into a bun. "For your information, I found a 'book of cookery' in the library and boiled the cheese the proper way. Then I sampled it to make sure we wouldn't die." She smacked her lips as if remembering the taste. "It wasn't half-bad."

I regarded her shrewdly, then shrugged. "Okay, I've never had homemade cheese. Why not?"

"Great!" said Mom, opening the bedroom door. "And we can . . . ACK!" She tumbled face-first into the hallway.

"Mom!" I ran to help her up. "Are you okay?"

She twisted onto her backside, and I could see a long, narrow box underneath her legs. Someone had positioned it just outside our bedroom door.

"What's that?" I asked, kneeling beside her.

"A mother slaying device," she said, taking the hand I offered.

We both faced the box, which was latched on the front with a simple turn clasp.

"What do you think's inside?" I asked.

"Only one way to find out."

Mom popped open the lid, and we peered into the box. Two beribboned scrolls sat on top of a set of metal cuffs that had iron balls attached with chains.

"This doesn't look promising," she said, trying to heft one of the balls out of the box.

I grabbed a scroll and slipped off the ribbon. Written inside the curled paper was a note.

To Whoever Selected This Scroll:

It appears you're still in the contest, thriving like the majestic cockroach.

It is now my pleasure to inform you that you've developed beriberi, a common colonial illness that, left untreated, will cripple your muscles and kill you.

I lowered the paper and looked at Mom. "I have beriberi."

"Sounds delicious," she said. "Maybe we can make cobbler-cobbler."

I shook my head. "This isn't funny! It's a disease that's going to kill me!"

Mom gave me a withering look. "I'll admit Great-Aunt Muriel was mean, but she wouldn't kill any of us. She couldn't legally get away with it."

"What does *she* care? She's dead!"

Mom took the letter from me. "You didn't read the whole thing." Clearing her throat, she continued:

Since, sadly, I could not afflict you with the actual illness, this is only a hypothetical scenario. The ankle weights will simulate your muscle depletion. Don them as soon as you finish this letter. If you "die" from the disease before the sun sets, you might as well go home.

"It's like getting a hug from her," I mumbled, hefting one of the balls and chains out of the box. Mom helped me fasten it around my ankle. "What did the other scroll say?"

"That I have a family member afflicted with beriberi," she

said, making a face. "And that I have until sunset to find the cure."

"Great."

I fastened the second weight around my other ankle and gripped the doorframe as I got to my feet. I took a few test steps, the lead balls slowing me to a snail's pace.

I turned to Mom. "Please cure me fast."

She nodded, a determined look in her eye. "Thank goodness I've been watching those medical shows."

"I don't think *Moles Shaped Like Animals* is considered a medical show," I said, literally dragging my feet until I was in front of Angel's door. There was no box sitting outside *her* room.

After three knocks, she answered with a carrot in hand.

"What's up, Doc?"

"Aw, man! Why aren't *you* dying?" I asked.

Angel raised an eyebrow. "Sorry?"

I shook my head. "I caught this disease called beriberi—"

Angel took a giant step back.

"It's not real!" I said. "But Mom only has until sunset to find the cure or we're out."

Angel paused mid–carrot crunch. "Yikes. I would *not* want to be in your"—she looked down—"ankle cuffs."

"Well, do you know anything about beriberi?" I asked.

She shook her head. "Try looking in the library. Or asking your boyfriend."

For a moment, I was taken aback. "I can't do that! It's cheating." Then the second part of her words sunk in, and I giggled. "And shut up. He's not my boyfriend!" I smacked her arm.

Angel rolled her eyes. "Well, whatever your plan, you'd better hurry."

I glanced from her to my ankle.

She cleared her throat. "So to speak."

"Did you at least get *any* kind of illness this morning?" I asked.

She shrugged. "There was a note tacked to my door that said I had a headache, but I chewed on some willow bark, and Eli told me I was cured."

I sighed. "Of course he did."

I did a quick check up and down the hall. Nobody else had a box outside their door either.

"Mom and I must have been really lucky that we got selected for this," I said in a flat voice.

"You'll figure it out," she said. "Good luck."

After Angel closed her door, I called to Mom, who ducked under one of my arms, and the two of us clambered downstairs as fast as my failing muscles would allow.

"Looks like there's a hitch in your giddyup," said Uncle Max from the dining room table. "You being punished?"

I spotted Eli watching us with a smug expression.

"You could say that," I told Uncle Max.

Mom disappeared to make breakfast, and I leaned toward Uncle Max. "Have you ever heard of beriberi?"

His forehead wrinkled. "Is that a new boy band?"

I settled back in my chair. "Never mind."

Mom returned with my food, and I held up the plate for Eli to see. "Is *this* the cure for beriberi?"

He shook his head. "Nay. None of those foods will do."

I shrugged at Mom. "Worth a shot."

She cleared her throat and cocked her head toward the kitchen.

Caleb was coming in through the door, his eyes fixed on his father even though I sat mere feet from his path.

"Hey, Caleb," I said.

He ignored me.

Mom put her fingers in her mouth and let out a piercing whistle.

Everyone turned, startled.

"Caleb, my daughter was greeting you," she said. "Surely colonial manners don't include ignoring a sweet girl whose mother is the one you should really be upset with."

Both Caleb and I blushed, and he mumbled something before hurrying from the room.

It was Mom's turn to shrug. "I *tried*."

I squeezed her arm. "Thanks. Let's go to the library and hit the books."

"Reading?" Eli laughed. "There is no time for leisure during the day. There is work to be done!"

Mom and I shot him dismayed looks.

"What?" Mom asked.

"How are we supposed to find a cure if we don't have time to look for one?" I asked.

Eli waved away my concern. "While you are still mobile, it is your duty to pull your weight in the family."

"I *am* pulling weight!" I pointed to my ankle. "Why—"

"The morning's challenge is about to begin!" Eli bellowed for all to hear. Then he walked out the back door.

"I get the feeling he doesn't like us," said Mom.

The morning's challenge turned out to require a lot of running.

"I get the feeling he *really* doesn't like us," I told Mom while Eli gave the instructions.

Since fires were left burning in colonial homes during the day, there were bound to be accidents where they got out of hand. Our task was to fill a barrel with ten buckets of water as quickly as possible, extinguishing an imaginary fire.

But because the full buckets were so heavy, they required two people to carry them, which meant that even if Mom sprinted to fetch the water, I still had to help her carry it back.

"How much you want to bet Eli just came up with this challenge last night?" I mumbled to Mom.

The minute he gave the word, I wrapped an arm around Mom's shoulder and we hobbled as quickly as we could to the water pump while people raced past us. When we reached the pump, we were alone since everyone else had already headed back with their first load of water. Mom let go of me so she could fill the bucket, and I tried to step out of her way.

And immediately fell down.

Mom turned to see what had happened and tripped over one of my lead weights, sloshing half her bucket of water on me.

"Glub!" I protested and sputtered.

"Sorry, honey. Looks like you got a free shower." Mom pulled me to my feet and went back to filling the bucket.

I heard laughter and glared in Eli's direction. Caleb stood beside him but didn't join in his father's mirth.

"Hey." Mom nudged me. "Let's go."

I grabbed one of the bucket's handles, and Mom held the other. Then she took four quick steps forward. I tried to catch up, but my weights dragged through the grass, the chains pulling tight until I stumbled to my knees. My hand was still on the bucket, and it jerked downward so that the bucket tilted crazily and half the water dumped out.

"Oh, come on!" I shouted.

More laughter, muffled behind one of Eli's meaty hands. Caleb continued to stare, looking anxious. Or possibly guilty?

Around us, people continued to race back and forth.

"I think it'll just be easier if we fill the buckets halfway and I go it alone," said Mom.

"But that's double the trips," I told her, getting to my feet.

"Sweetie, we haven't even made *one* trip." She pulled the bucket from my grasp and hurried away.

I sighed and sat on the back of an empty cart.

Then I gasped and stood up.

"Mom!" I shouted, reaching down for one of my lead weights. The chain was just long enough for me to load it into the cart. I hoisted the second one in after it. Then I grabbed the handles of the cart and pushed it to the water pump to meet her.

"That's brilliant!" she cried, placing the full bucket into the cart next to my weights. We both pushed, making it across the yard almost as fast as everyone else.

There was no more laughter from the sidelines.

Mom and I didn't finish first, but we didn't finish dead last, avoiding elimination.

"We have to find a way to research the cure," I told her once we were back inside starting our chores. "Leisure time isn't until after sunset, and by then it'll be too late."

She nodded. "You stay here where Eli can see you, and struggle as much as you can. Really put on a show. I'll sneak off to the library and see what I can find out."

"What if he asks where you are?"

"Tell him I'm sick," Mom whispered. "It wouldn't be far from the truth. I think the homemade cheese was a bad idea."

"Gross." I wrinkled my nose. "Good luck with . . . everything."

Eli was outside talking with Caleb, so I took a bar of soap and some rags and dragged my weights out to join them.

"Time to do some cleaning!" I chirped happily. "Boy, that was embarrassing what happened to me earlier, huh? I hope I don't . . . whoa!"

I pretended to trip and tossed the rags wildly about me. Eli pressed his lips together, but the glee in his eyes was obvious. I started to gather the rags and then sneezed into the dirt so that it flew in my face. I coughed for real and wiped at my sweaty brow until the dirt turned to a thin coat of mud.

The things I'd do to win a stupid contest.

Eli let a snicker escape. But Caleb scowled and stormed off to his craft hut.

Eli and I stared after him and then at each other.

"I don't know if that was about you or me," I said.

"*I* did nothing wrong," said Eli, pushing past me and heading for the barn.

Putting down the rags and soap, I dragged my weights over to the craft hut and cracked the door open. Caleb glanced up from something he was working on but didn't say anything.

"You didn't like my tumbling routine?" I asked. "Because my mom and I were thinking about adding it to our comedy show."

Instead of smiling, his dark expression deepened.

"Don't talk about your mom to me. She humiliated my family."

"You know she didn't mean anything by it. She was just trying to save *my* family." I started to approach the table but jerked to a halt when one of the lead balls got caught in the doorframe. Caleb reached down and helped me clear it.

"Still, it was really embarrassing," he said. "And a lot of people are questioning us now. My mom won't leave the house because she hates the whispering."

I chewed my lip. "I'm sorry she feels that way, but in case you haven't noticed, I'm not exactly having it easy either." I lifted a leg, and the chains rattled.

Caleb frowned and hung his head. "What my dad's doing isn't fair," he said. "I know he's upset, but he's handling it the wrong way." Caleb reached for one of my dirt-covered hands. "And I don't want to see you get hurt or humiliated anymore." He poked his head outside before closing the door and turning back to me. "The cure for beriberi is simple. It's—"

"LA!" I screamed, shoving my fingers in my ears. "LALA-LALALALA!"

Caleb looked taken aback and mouthed something to me.

"You can't give me the answer!" I shouted. "It's cheating!"

He tilted his head to one side and started to speak again.

"No!" I said. "You could get in trouble for helping me. Promise you won't."

Caleb sighed and nodded. I took my fingers out of my ears.

"Look, I didn't come for answers or to make you feel worse," I said. "I came to make sure we could still be friends. My mom and I would *never* intentionally hurt someone, and I'm sure if she knew how bad this made your family feel, she'd be apologizing in person."

Caleb crossed his arms. "Why isn't she?"

"Because she's in the library trying to find a way to cure me," I said. "Except she won't have much longer if your dad finds her."

He shook his head. "Don't worry about that. I'll talk to my dad."

"Thanks." I smiled at him. "I'd hug you, but it would take a while to get there."

Caleb laughed and took a few steps closer. But instead of hugging me, he leaned in and gave me the quickest kiss on the lips. When he stepped back, he wiped his mouth.

My heart sank into my shackles. "That bad?"

"There was a lot of dirt," he said, grinning. He dipped a rag in the metal-cooling barrel and dabbed at my face until the stiffness of the mud disappeared. Then he kissed me again. "Much better."

I smiled. "I should go help my mom. If I die, you and I can't hang out anymore."

Caleb walked me to the door. "I could give you the answer," he reminded me.

"I know," I said, blowing him a kiss. Then I slowly made my way back into the house.

The library was just past the kitchen, but when I approached the entrance, I didn't hear the usual mumblings of my mom talking to herself. The room was completely quiet.

Too quiet.

I poked my head inside.

Mom was fast asleep in an armchair by the window. There

was a stack of books by her feet with a cup of tea resting on top.

"Again?! You have *got* to be kidding me," I growled. "Mom!"

She didn't budge . . . just snored.

I bent down and removed a shoe. Then I chucked it at her.

"Mom!" The shoe struck her in the leg, but she mumbled something about unicorns and kept right on napping.

I approached her and prodded her. One eye opened and rolled around to take in the whole room. Then it closed and she slumbered on.

"Nice to know I can count on you in an emergency," I mumbled, shifting the teacup to the floor and grabbing the top book.

The table of contents made no mention of beriberi, but it talked about cures for common ailments. I flipped through the pages and looked at remedies: spearmint for indigestion, lavender for sleeplessness, pine for scurvy . . . but nothing about beriberi.

The sun moved past the window as I continued to search through medical books but found nothing. Soon my stomach began to growl. I thought back to breakfast longingly.

Then I thought about when I'd asked if my eggs and cheese were a cure for beriberi. Eli had said none of *those* foods would do it.

Which meant *some* food would be the cure.

I returned to the bookshelves and grabbed anything I could find that referenced food in the title. I didn't even bother organizing. My sweaty fingers turned the pages, too aware of the shortage of time as my eyes squinted to adjust to the fading sun.

I'd just about lost hope when, in a book about rice, the author mentioned how the rice shouldn't have the husk removed. Doing so would take away the thiamin content, resulting in beriberi.

"That's it!" I got to my feet and turned toward the doorway. To my surprise, a small crowd had gathered to watch, including Eli.

"Thiamin!" I shouted. "I need foods rich in thiamin, like unhulled rice!"

Eli regarded me with a look of contempt. "We do not have rice in this section of the world."

"Legumes have a lot of thiamin," commented Aunt Zoe. "And there are plenty here."

Eli whirled to face her. If looks could kill . . .

"Legumes, then!" I shouted. "I'd eat some legumes . . . once I figure out what they are."

"Peanuts, dear," said Aunt Zoe. "And beans."

"Stop helping her!" shouted Dylan. "That's cheating!"

I looked to Eli. "All the note said was that we had to find the cure before sunset."

He opened and closed his mouth several times and blustered before finally barking, "You're cured!" and fuming away. People followed him, muttering words of disappointment.

Our Christmas card list would definitely be cut down this year.

"Who's being loud?" Mom whined, and shifted in the chair to look at me. Then she seemed to realize where she was and sat bolt upright. "The cure! I've got—"

"No, *I've* got," I told her, removing the cuffs from my ankles. "No thanks to you."

Mom paused while rubbing her eyes. "Hey, I was in here all day—"

"Sleeping," I finished. "While I, once again, had to be the grown-up and fix everything."

"I didn't mean to fall asleep," Mom protested, still talking. "I just had some tea with Angel and then came in here and . . ." She narrowed her eyes, my words finally sinking in. "Excuse me?"

"I'm always the responsible one!" I blurted before I could stop myself. "You never step up and act like an adult. Which is why we're even in this stupid contest, about to lose our home."

Mom's face darkened to a storm cloud. "Oh, you'd better

take that back right now, little girl. The only thing I should be getting from you is gratitude for giving you life and keeping you alive every day."

"Keeping me alive?" I repeated with a sharp laugh. "How many times have your clever ideas almost gotten me hurt or killed? I'd be better off on my own."

I could see the muscles in Mom's jaw clench and hear her labored breathing, as if it were taking every ounce of her strength *not* to throw a couch across the room. Finally, Mom threw her hands up. "Fine! Bye. I hope you can find someone who puts up with your incessant nagging and dream killing."

I just stood there for a moment, stunned by the harshness of her words. Mom had *never* said such mean things about me. Good moms weren't supposed to.

"I hate you! You're a terrible mom!" I shouted at her.

Her face softened as her expression slipped from anger to pain. Before she could even say anything, I sprinted from the room and out onto the property. Anywhere to get away from the worst mother in the world.

Chapter Twelve

At that particular moment, there were only two voices I would have stopped for. One of them called out to me.

"Tori! Wait a sec!"

I stopped on the edge of the cornfield so Angel could catch up.

"I heard you found the cure. Congrats!"

"Thanks," I said with a tight smile.

She studied my face. "What's wrong? You should be thrilled."

"Thrilled that my mom can't be relied on for even the simple task of reading?" I snorted, and started walking farther from the manor.

Angel matched my pace.

"She hasn't been all bad," she said. "She got the horses back from Dylan, she saved you when you threw fuel on the fire. . . ."

"The worst part," I interrupted, "is I didn't even get to eat lunch, so there's no way I'll be ready for tonight's challenge."

Angel reached into a satchel she'd slung across her body. "Here."

She fished out a bundled cloth and handed it to me. Inside was a pile of plump blueberries.

"Oooh . . . I love you!" I told her. "Where did you find them?"

She pointed to the woods just beyond the cornfield. "There are bushes overgrown with them. I figured Mother Nature wouldn't mind if I helped myself."

I popped a handful in my mouth. "You are amazing. I wish I had survival skills like yours."

Angel shrugged and did her best to look modest. "I guess my parents rubbed off a little."

I swallowed and headed into the forest. "I want some more."

Angel gave me a dubious frown. "The challenge will be coming up soon."

"Exactly. And I need sustenance. I'll pick some real quick, and then we'll go back."

She nodded. "Okay, real quick."

"Make a path," I told her as we pushed into the woods. Dozens of blueberries went from the stem to my mouth as we walked.

"Do you have an extra cloth I can put more in?" I asked. Even if I was mad at Mom, I knew she'd love some berries too.

Angel reached into her satchel again, removing a small handful of items. "Nope. Nothing I can spare."

I looked at the items she clutched in her hand. Among them were some purple flowers.

"Is that lavender?" I asked, taking a sprig and sniffing.

"Uh . . . yeah." Angel put everything back in her bag. "I found some growing wild and thought I'd put them in my room. Pretty, right?"

I stared at the petals for a moment.

"Tori?"

"How did you know I threw fuel on the fire?" I locked my eyes on Angel's. "Mom and I didn't tell anyone, and we were the only ones outside when it happened."

Angel blinked at me. "I heard Dylan bragging about his prank."

I shook my head. "He wouldn't admit to sabotage. It might cost him the game."

She shrugged. "Well, I found out somehow."

I held up the lavender. "I read about this today. Do you know what it's used for?"

Angel shifted the weight of the satchel on her hip. "Sometimes people use it in cooking."

"Cooking tea?" I asked her. "Cooking tea that puts people to sleep?"

"I guess. . . . " Angel grabbed my arm. "We should really get back to the others."

"You!" I jerked free of her grasp. "All this time, *you* were the one sabotaging me and my mom. Not Dylan!"

Angel forced a laugh. "Tori, don't be ridiculous! I'd never do anything like that."

"Sure you would," I said, my mouth set in a line. "You really want your mom and dad to get off your case about living the natural life. You hate it. If you don't win this, they're just going to make you try even harder when you get home."

Angel shook her head twice and then let out a huge sigh. "Fine! I was the one sabotaging you and your mom. And yes, I really need to win this. You have no idea how insufferable my parents are going to be otherwise!"

"Unbelievable!" I threw the lavender sprig at her. "You know how bad my mom and I need the money! How could you?"

Angel twisted her hands together. "Tori—"

"Don't talk to me, you . . . you *witch*. If we lose this and my mom loses her business, it's all on you!" I turned around, took five steps to the right, and paused.

"I still think you're a witch, but . . . which is the way out?"

Angel squinted and pursed her lips. "I think . . . that way?"

She pointed at a path so overgrown with foliage, there was no way we'd just come through it.

"Fine, if you want to keep playing your little game." I crossed my arms. "I'll just go wherever you go."

Angel shot me a dirty look and then stepped past me. I followed her in silence as we climbed over logs and swept plants aside. At one point she stopped and I noticed something on the ground.

"Is one of your legs shorter than the other?" I asked.

Angel sighed. "Why, Tori?"

"Because we just walked in a huge circle." I pointed down at the lavender sprig I'd thrown at her earlier.

Angel stared at it. "Huh. We may be lost."

"What?!" I cried loud enough to startle a nearby bird from a tree. "I thought I told you to make a path!"

Angel looked at me, wide-eyed. "I thought you said 'makeup app'!"

"*Why* would I say 'makeup app'?"

"Because I like makeup and I miss technology!" Angel screeched.

I tilted my head back and tried to see a patch of sky, hoping to figure out where the sun was, but the ceiling was nothing but tree branches and darkness. "Okay, well, use your survival skills to get us out of here."

Angel stood transfixed.

"Please tell me you're recalling survival knowledge and *not* peeing yourself," I said.

"I can't get us out of here," she whispered. "I get lost at the mall."

I sighed and rubbed my eyes. "Is that why you went for a pretzel once and came back with a security guard and a balloon?"

Angel nodded. "I don't have any survival skills. My parents have been doing it all. They're the ones who told me about the blueberry bushes."

I dropped into a crouch and took several deep, calming breaths. We needed to approach the situation logically. "The good news is that we can't be too far from the property, so someone will eventually find us."

"And the bad news?"

"We might be dead when they do."

Angel whimpered. "I miss my phone. It has maps. And the number for the security guard at the mall."

"Yeah, I don't think he'd be able to help us navigate the

woods, so we have to think." I studied the trees around us. "Is there any way besides the sun to tell which direction we are?"

"The stars," said Angel.

"I don't want to be here after dark," I said. "Anything else?"

She shook her head. "Nothing that doesn't require sunlight."

I thought for a moment, but nothing from my schoolbooks came to mind, and the only idea I could come up with was to wait for help.

"What would my mom do?" I muttered.

"She'd probably climb into the trees and live there," said Angel. "Start a new dress shop, making leaf fashions for the woodland critters."

I smiled. "Learn to speak chipmunk."

"Maybe a little goose," said Angel, pointing overhead. Somewhere above the forest a flock honked as it flew past.

I gripped her arm and gasped. "That's it! It's summertime!"

Angel looked at me quizzically and then suddenly mirrored my excitement. "Geese fly south in the winter, then back north in the summer!"

We quieted and listened intently to the birds.

"That way." We both pointed the same direction and triumphantly began our return to the manor.

Even though I'd said I didn't want to be out after dark, the sun began to set and it became harder to see in front of us.

We were forced to rely on vague tree shapes to know where we were going.

Until we saw the lights sweeping from side to side. They were accompanied by voices. Several.

"Mom?" I shouted.

The voices stopped, and then, "Tori! Tori, thank God. Where are you?"

"And is Angel with you?" There was no mistaking Aunt Zoe's anxious voice.

"I'm here!" called Angel. She sounded close to tears.

I found her hand, and we moved quicker toward where we'd heard the others.

"Keep talking so we can find you!" I shouted.

"I'm so sorry, Tori!" called Mom. "You were right to be upset with me. I've been failing you this whole time."

A lump formed in my throat. "No, you haven't!" I wheezed in a voice that was breathless with exertion and emotion. "You've been doing incredible things that I never could. You always have been."

Silence from outside the woods.

"Mom?"

"Just get out here so I can hug you," she said in a choked voice.

Finally, *finally*, there was a break in the trees and we could see bright beams of light and shadowed figures behind them. Several of the lights dropped to the ground, their owners blotting out light from the others as they dashed toward Angel and me.

"Tori!" Mom threw her arms open and wrapped me in a bear hug.

It was the best hug I'd ever had. Even though we both smelled like public toilets.

"I'm sorry I said all those mean things," I said.

"I deserved them," she said. "I shouldn't have fallen asleep when something so important was at stake."

I pulled away from Mom. "It's okay. It wasn't your fault."

I turned toward Angel, who was still hugging her parents but had twisted her head toward me, eyes wide with uncertainty. Ever so subtly, she shook her head, but I couldn't let her take advantage of us anymore.

"Mom." I took her hands. "Someone put lavender in your tea to make you fall asleep. The same person who added fuel to our water and spilled our cornmeal and did all those other nasty things."

For a moment, Mom's forehead wrinkled. Then the wrinkles shifted to frown lines and she spun around to glare at Dylan and Uncle Max.

"You?!"

"No, no." I tugged her fingers. "Dylan wasn't the bad guy. It was . . . " I couldn't bring myself to say the words, so I just nodded my head in Angel's direction.

At first, Uncle Deke and Aunt Zoe glanced around in confusion, wondering who I could be talking about. And then Aunt Zoe gasped, mouth hanging open.

"Wait . . . " said Uncle Deke. He held his daughter at arm's length. "Angel?"

Instantly, her gaze dropped to the ground.

"It was me," she said in a soft voice.

Everyone in the crowd was suddenly abuzz, especially Dylan.

"You thought I did those things? I'm offended!"

I glanced past Mom. "I'm so sorry, Dylan."

"I would've come up with *much* better ways to destroy you," he finished.

"And now I'm less sorry," I said.

"This is quite the game changer," said another voice.

I jumped in surprise, not realizing Eli was among the search party.

"We must away to the manor and discuss what needs be done," he said.

"Will my family be disqualified?" asked Angel in a meek voice.

"That is not for me to decide," said Eli. He motioned for the rest of us to follow. "Come. Judgment awaits."

Mom kept her arm linked through mine the entire time, as if she were afraid I'd suddenly vanish, but she was also humming. I couldn't blame her. Now that we were reunited and the truth was out about the sabotage, it felt like we were that much closer to victory. Except . . .

I ground to a halt, jerking Mom back with me. "How did you do by yourself at the evening challenge?"

Mom snorted. "Really? You think we just kept on competing while two little girls were missing?"

"I'm not a little girl!" I said, pinching her side.

Mom kissed the top of my head. "You'll always be my little girl."

Behind us, Angel didn't seem to be having quite the same bonding moment with her parents. I couldn't hear every word, but Uncle Deke and Aunt Zoe were definitely laying into her, and I heard "dangerous" used more than once. I supposed they were right. What if Mom had been allergic to lavender? Or one of us had been burned in the fuel incident?

I didn't envy Angel whatever came next. I had a feeling it involved a call to Great-Aunt Muriel's lawyer or perhaps even the police.

When we were in earshot of the manor, Eli waved to his

wife, who had emerged from hiding to pace the backyard. She stopped when she saw her husband and ducked her head into the house to yell to Caleb. Then she bustled toward us as fast as her lifted skirts would allow.

"Blessed be, you're all right!" She smiled at me, but when she turned to Angel with the same greeting, her smile wavered. She took in Angel's sullen expression and the irritated ones of Aunt Zoe and Uncle Deke.

"Eli, what has happened to this one?" she asked.

"We have a problem," he told her.

Just then Caleb burst into view wearing a broad grin.

"Tori! You're safe!" He hugged me.

In front of everyone.

Including his parents.

The crowd's reactions were almost as explosive as they'd been for Angel, except Mom, who sighed and said, "Oh, Tori."

"It appears I misspoke," hissed Eli with venom in his voice. "We have *two* problems."

He pulled Caleb away from me and pushed his son toward the servants' quarters. "Wait there. And enjoy every breath as if it were your last. Because it might be."

"Please don't punish him!" I said. "It's my fault anything happened. I was the one who broke the rules."

"Oh, I am well aware of that," said Eli. "And you will suffer the consequences." He bowed his head and sighed. "I suppose it's too much to ask for honesty in this day and age. You seemed like good, decent children."

It was mine and Angel's turns to bow our heads.

I didn't try to persuade Eli any further, and he didn't speak another word or even look at us as he led Angel and me and our parents into the house. His wife at least squeezed my arm reassuringly as we passed her.

Eli opened the door to a large study and finally spoke.

"Wait here while I contact the judge to decide your fate."

Angel took one couch with her parents, while Mom and I took the other.

As soon as Eli closed the door, I faced Mom and began babbling, "I'm so sorry! I've doomed us to a life of poverty. We'll have to close the dress shop and live in a refrigerator box and use the fabric to make tiny curtains for the cutout windows and—"

Mom cupped my face in both hands. "Tori. It's okay. You're a good kid, but I can't expect you to be perfect all the time."

I nodded and leaned forward with my arms around my knees, making myself as small as possible.

"Besides," said Mom, "I knew you and Caleb were crushing on each other, and I could've interfered at any time."

"Could've?" I twisted to glance at her. "You made me sleep in the barn!"

From across the room, Aunt Zoe let out a tiny laugh that she quickly covered with a cough.

"And clearly that didn't work," said Mom. "I should've done something more extreme. Like make you sleep in the footlocker with the chickens."

"Chickens?" asked Uncle Deke. "You have chickens in your room?"

"*Had*," I corrected. "They met a grisly fate."

"That's what all the squawking was!" Aunt Zoe elbowed him. "I told you they could sing better than that."

"Hey!" Mom and I said at the same time, but by now we were all smiling, even Angel.

"I don't think they've ever heard our rendition of 'Don't Stop Believin', " Mom said to me.

"You'll have to treat us to a performance one of these days," said Uncle Deke.

The doorknob clicked, and we all stopped talking and sat up straight. Eli appeared, red faced and somber.

"Ladies and gentleman," he said, "the judge would like to speak with you in person."

"Right . . . right now?" asked Mom, raising an eyebrow.

Eli nodded. "Considering the severity of the situation, we thought it best. Is that acceptable?"

"It doesn't matter if they find it acceptable—it's my contest!" croaked a voice from somewhere behind him.

That voice.

Even though I'd only heard it a handful of times, it was unforgettable. And from the awestruck expressions on the faces of my family, I knew I was right.

Eli winced as a marble-headed cane smacked him in the arm.

"Step aside, you blundering buffoon! Or should I speak *through* you, like a ventriloquist working a dummy?"

A tiny white-haired woman tottered past him and fixed us all with her steely eyes.

"What's the matter?" asked Great-Aunt Muriel with a sly grin. "You all look like you've seen a ghost."

Chapter Thirteen

Eli helped Great-Aunt Muriel into a chair and then stood against a wall with his arms crossed.

Great-Aunt Muriel's chin wobbled a bit, and her hands shook as she rested her cane in her lap. But her voice was hardened and forceful.

"You have all been staring at me with open mouths since I arrived. How many flies do you expect to catch?"

Almost in unison, everyone clamped their mouths shut. Except Aunt Zoe.

"Great-Aunt Muriel," she said, taking a tiny step forward. "I'm sorry to point this out, but we thought . . . " She gestured

vaguely at Great-Aunt Muriel's fragile form. Then she turned
to Uncle Deke.

"We received letters stating that you had passed away," he
supplied.

"I'm aware," said Great-Aunt Muriel. "I'm the one who
sent them."

"But why?" asked Mom.

Great-Aunt Muriel raised a white eyebrow. "If anyone in
this room should be asking questions, do you really think it's
you?" She raised her cane and pointed the tip of it at me. "You."
She swung the cane toward Angel. "And you. Come here."

Angel made a tiny whimpering noise and stepped forward. I
took a deep breath and did the same. Angel scooted as close to
me as possible without actually melding her body with mine.

"That's sweet," Great-Aunt Muriel said with a stony
expression. "You sidle up to the one you betrayed. Is that why
you sabotaged her? Because of your boundless respect?"

Angel's face crinkled, and she burst into tears.

Great-Aunt Muriel sighed and reached for a tissue box,
holding it with one shaky hand. "My dear," she said, "tears
are for tragedies. And this is not one."

Nevertheless, Angel kept crying and intermittently apologizing through a mixture of snot and waterworks. Great-Aunt
Muriel just watched.

"Imagine," she said, "if we could consider the consequences of our actions *before* we took them." She turned to
me. "Although I expect *you* already knew. You disobeyed the
rules anyway. Why?" Her eyes narrowed. "And if you say 'for
love,' I will feed you to Charity. She bit another horse once
and has developed a taste for flesh."

I swallowed hard. "Because Caleb and I have so much in
common. I don't really connect with anyone my age."

Great-Aunt Muriel leaned forward on her cane. "What do
you have in common?"

"We both like school, we both work hard, and . . . " I
blushed, feeling guilty for what I was about to say. "We both
come from families that are struggling with money, and we
wish we could do more to help."

Out of the corner of my eye, I could see Eli shift against
the wall. I chanced a glimpse back at Mom, who smiled with
moist eyes.

"Also, we're not into all the trendy, popular stuff like most
kids."

Great-Aunt Muriel rolled her eyes. "People who follow
trends are as preposterous as the trends themselves. I prefer
you the way you are."

A warm glow filled my chest. "Really? But you hardly know
anything about me."

"I know plenty," she said. "I've been watching all of you throughout this contest."

I gasped and snapped my fingers. "That was *your* video camera I found in the tree!"

She nodded. "I was afraid someone would figure that out, and luckily it was Elias." She gave Eli an approving smile. "And he was quick and clever enough to distract the rest of you with a witch trial."

Eli stood a little taller and prouder, and I couldn't help regarding him with more respect.

"To get back to the matter at hand," said Great-Aunt Muriel, "Victoria, *you* possess a fiery determination that I admire. You were given several opportunities to cheat, yet you never did. Such integrity is rare in a world where people will do anything to get ahead."

Angel cleared her throat and studied the carpet. "Like me."

I was afraid Great-Aunt Muriel might scold her again, but instead she said, "Though I don't condone your acts of sabotage, Angel, they were clever, and managing to convince even adults to assume the wrong culprit was nothing short of genius."

Great-Aunt Muriel curled a finger at Angel to beckon her closer. When Angel was within a foot of her chair, Great-Aunt Muriel winked at her.

"But I believe you will get further in life if you are truthful with your parents . . . and yourself. Do you understand?"

Angel nodded, tears filling her eyes again. She opened her mouth to speak, but Great-Aunt Muriel held up a hand.

"You have apologized enough to cover yourself and every prisoner in Sing Sing. I simply ask for honesty."

Mom, who had been silent up until this point, finally spoke. "If it's not too much to ask, maybe *we* could get a little honesty now?"

Great-Aunt Muriel leaned around Angel and me to look at Mom.

"I see where your daughter gets her doggedness. Very well. Elias, will you fetch us some tea and biscuits from my private collection? I find they go best with jaw-dropping revelations." She gestured to the rest of us. "Sit if you wish to stay. My neck has enough difficulty supporting my head without having to stare up at you behemoths."

"You make it sound like you're a newborn baby," I said, settling on the carpet in front of her chair.

She smirked. "I suppose that's an accurate analogy. My muscles are underdeveloped, my motor skills are poor, and soon I'll be eating soft foods and muttering incomprehensible things."

"You make old age sound like a dream," said Mom.

Everyone laughed.

"There are benefits, to be certain," said Great-Aunt Muriel. "For example, I can speak however I choose, and people simply attribute it to old age instead of my personality."

Everyone laughed again.

I nudged Mom, who was sitting beside me. "We should try telling people you're old next time you flip out at a buffet."

"*Why* can't I put a slice of cake back and get one with more frosting?" she demanded.

"You *can* . . . if you haven't taken a bite out of it yet!" I said.

Great-Aunt Muriel watched us, fascinated. "How the two of you are still alive and not missing limbs is a mystery."

Eli returned, wheeling a cart laden with a tea set. Felicity followed with a platter containing cookies and two items wrapped in paper.

"I thought the girls might be a little hungry after their wilderness adventure," she said, handing a package to each of us. I reached for mine, and she held on to it for a second, meeting my eye before letting go. Everyone else was too focused on the tea service to notice.

"Thank you," I said, opening the sandwich wrapper. When I lifted out a half, I noticed something scribbled on the paper underneath. I quickly tilted it so nobody else could see, stuffing one part of the sandwich in my mouth and lifting out the other.

> Tori, I'm really, really, REALLY sorry. I hope you aren't in too much trouble. If you don't hate me, please meet me at the barn so I can apologize in person.
>
> Caleb

Mom nudged me. "What's so fascinating about that sandwich?"

I was about to say, "Nothing." But then I realized she deserved better than that. So I held the wrapper where she could see.

Mom's eyes flitted from side to side as she read. Then they closed entirely.

"Tori," she said with a sigh.

"I didn't say I was going," I whispered.

"Porter Family?" Eli towered over us, holding out two cups of tea with sugar cubes and spoons resting on their saucers.

"Thank you," said Mom, reaching up to take them.

Eli started to move on, but I grabbed his pant leg.

"I'm sorry," I said.

Eli glanced down in surprise.

"I'm sorry we let you down."

For the first time ever, Eli's face softened. "I shouldn't be so hard on you. You *are* young, ruled more by your hearts than your heads. And my son has been very happy since your arrival."

I beamed up at him. "He has?"

Eli nodded. "I assumed it was excitement for the contest, but . . . as I say, youth is ruled by the heart." He smiled and moved on, and again I felt a warm glow inside me.

Once the tinkling of spoons in teacups had stopped and everyone was settled comfortably, Great-Aunt Muriel took a long sip and began.

"It is true, I'm *not* dead, as is evidenced by my presence, but you all seem to be wondering why not. The fact of the matter is, I'm not dead, but I *am* dying. The doctors give me approximately one month to live." Great-Aunt Muriel's face remained passive, as if she'd already accepted this truth.

"What are you dying from?" I asked.

"You don't assume it's because I'm old?" she asked with a wry smile.

"From the stories we hear, you seem pretty indestructible," said Angel.

"The Unsinkable Muriel Archibald, eh?" She chuckled. "If you must know, I'm dying from a combination of old age, asbestos, and uranium."

"Uranium?" asked Uncle Deke. "When would you have come into contact with nuclear materials?"

She pressed her lips together. "I have not been entirely forthright about my past. It is true I worked in the steel industry, but it wasn't for a privately funded company."

"For who, then?" asked Mom.

"The US government," said Great-Aunt Muriel. "My white-collar job was a cover for my work in counterespionage."

"Espionage," I repeated. "You were a *spy*?"

"That's so cool!" said Angel. "Did you have a grappling gun?"

She and I were now both leaning forward, food forgotten.

Great-Aunt Muriel's shoulders shook with suppressed laughter. "Before you imagine me slinking about in a black jumpsuit, I can assure you my life was not so exciting. My duties were to gather overseas intelligence on those who were spying on *us*."

"That explains how you seem to know so much about our lives," said Mom with a smirk.

Great-Aunt Muriel tapped the side of her nose and pointed to Mom. "I've had decades of experience."

"And you couldn't think of even *one* family member to give your estate to?" Mom asked.

Great-Aunt Muriel took another sip of tea. "When I was a young girl, my family lived in abject poverty. My parents had five children, as you know, and I was the youngest. I was also the sickest and the weakest. There was never enough food to go around, and I got what little was left after my brothers and sisters had their fill."

I looked down at my sandwich, tempted to give it to Great-Aunt Muriel.

"One winter," she continued, "I caught a particularly bad case of pneumonia, but my parents couldn't afford to feed the family *and* get me a doctor."

"Oh," said Aunt Zoe, covering her mouth with her hand.

"And so they hoped that I would recover but focused their attention on their children who were still thriving."

I hugged my knees to my chest. Mom sidled closer and put an arm around me.

Great-Aunt Muriel watched us with a keen eye. "I've never quite understood the emphasis people place on family. Mine didn't make me a priority."

Her voice sounded almost wistful, and she reached over to put her teacup on a side table. It rattled in its saucer as she struggled to hold it.

"Let me get that," said Uncle Deke, taking it from her. She studied him.

"You're one of my sister Susanna's grandsons. Deke."

"That's right," he said with a smile.

"A name whose origin means 'servant,'" she continued. "How fitting that you offered to clear my dishware."

Uncle Deke dropped the smile.

I cleared my throat. "Maybe it would be easier to connect with family if you didn't give them reasons to disconnect?"

Great-Aunt Muriel looked at me. "If the man can't take a joke, it's a problem with *his* upbringing, not mine."

"It's fine," Uncle Deke told me. He turned his attention back to her. "So, if you don't feel close to any of your family, why bother offering an inheritance at all? Why not donate the estate to a historical society?"

Great-Aunt Muriel leaned forward on her cane. "Because as little as I believe in family, a tiny piece of me still does. Plus, I enjoy being amused, and hosting a contest is far more fascinating than anything on television. Have you seen what is deemed entertainment these days? Who cares what house-wives *anywhere* are doing?"

Everyone laughed.

"Just how many cameras have you had on us?" asked Aunt Zoe. "I haven't noticed any other than the one Tori found."

She squirmed uncomfortably. "And have they been watching *everything*?"

"I assure you, they were only placed in the common areas," said Great-Aunt Muriel, "and competition locales."

I frowned. "If you could see all that, then you must've seen Angel sabotaging my mom and me."

She tilted her hand from side to side. "As I said, she was cleverly subtle in her actions, and though I had a hunch she was up to something, I couldn't confirm it. I decided to leave it up to her competitors to spot."

Angel perked up. "Then since you don't really care, does that mean I'm not in trouble?"

Great-Aunt Muriel barked a laugh. "I never said I didn't care. You wouldn't be in this room if that were the case. No, you *will* be punished, as will Miss Porter."

"Really?" My shoulders slumped.

She regarded me with disbelief. "Well intended or not, deceit is deceit."

"So what *is* their punishment?" asked Mom, gripping my shoulder tighter.

"You needn't act as if I'm going to grind her up for chicken feed," said Great-Aunt Muriel. "I will simply disqualify both of them."

She said it so matter-of-factly that for a moment we all just continued to stare at her.

"Sorry," said Uncle Deke. "Disqualified?"

"Yes," said Great-Aunt Muriel. "Your children have been disqualified from the competition." She raised her voice over the sound of Angel and me protesting. "Since the adults are still eligible, the children may remain on the property in separate bedrooms. I feel that's a generous allowance."

"Or you could not disqualify me!" I said. "Seriously? Just because I talked to a guy?"

"Victoria," Mom said in a warning tone. "Don't press your luck."

Great-Aunt Muriel held up a hand. "It's all right. The fact of the matter is that she broke one of the main rules of this competition. No fraternizing with employees in case of unfair advantage."

"But I didn't have an unfair advantage!" I said. "Haven't you been watching me and my mom? We suck!"

"Hey," said Mom with a frown.

"I swear I didn't get any help," I continued. "You said so yourself; I had plenty of chances to cheat, and I didn't."

"Victoria," said Great-Aunt Muriel in a much calmer voice

than mine, "this decision is not up for debate."

"But my mom can't make it on her own!" I protested.

"Enough!" shouted Mom.

Everyone jumped, including Great-Aunt Muriel.

"I've taken as much of this as I can stand," said Mom, slamming her saucer and teacup on a table.

"Careful!" said Great-Aunt Muriel. "That's . . . "

Mom glared at her. "You can't take it with you, Muriel!" Then she pointed at me. "Ever since you found out we're in debt, you've seen nothing but the bad in all I do. You doubt me at every step. If there's *one* person in the world I hoped would trust me, it would be you."

I got to my feet. "Mom, I *do* trust—"

"You just said I can't make it on my own!" she bellowed.

"I meant . . . " I wrung my hands together.

She was right. Even after our conversation at the edge of the woods, I still didn't trust her to win for us. So many little things had gone wrong.

"Well?" She held her arms open while everyone else looked on. "What do you have to say for yourself?"

"I . . . well . . . " I turned to Great-Aunt Muriel. "Is the final challenge something related to shopping or celebrities?"

There was a bump to my shoulder as Mom pushed past me

to leave the room. "Good night, Tori. I'll leave your belongings in the hallway."

"Night," I said with a sigh.

Mom was furious and I was disqualified. But at least I
wasn't sleeping in the barn.

Chapter Fourteen

After the talk with Great-Aunt Muriel, I went upstairs and changed back into my street clothes. Now that I was no longer in the contest, it didn't really matter what I wore. And even though they weren't completely clean, these clothes smelled way better than my colonial ones.

Caleb was waiting right where he said he'd be, holding a bouquet of flowers and wearing a guilty expression. When he saw me, he jogged to close the distance between us.

"How epically did I screw up?" he asked. Then he did a double take at my outfit. "You're not in costume anymore!"

I took a deep breath and said, "I've been disqualified."

Caleb's eyes widened, then took on the same sternness as his father's. "I have to talk to Muriel and set things right," he said, marching past me.

"Caleb." I grabbed the crook of his elbow and stopped him. "Things *are* right."

He cocked an eyebrow at me.

"I deserve to be disqualified," I said. "Even if I didn't use my time with you to cheat in the contest, I still broke the rules."

Now that I was saying the facts out loud, I realized how true they were. I decided to try something.

"But it's okay," I continued. "My mom is going to do *great* on her own."

Caleb's eyebrows pushed together. "Why are you making a face like you drank bad milk?"

"Am I?" I said. "That's weird. I'm proud of my mom."

Caleb shook his head. "Now your face looks like you drank bad gasoline."

I smacked him with the flowers, and he eyed the petals falling to the ground.

"I'm glad I didn't give you a puppy. What's going on?" He held up a finger. "And don't say 'nothing,' because I'll bet the face that goes with *that* lie is even scarier."

I glared at him, and he blocked his body with his arms to deflect more floral abuse.

I lowered the bouquet to my side and stared past him. "I'm the worst daughter ever."

"Oh." Caleb frowned. "You really believe *that*. Why?" We started to walk around the property, hand in hand.

"I don't think my mom can win this on her own."

"Hm," he said. "I can see that. She *is up* against some pretty tough competitors, and they all have teams of at least two."

I shook my head. "No, it's not that. I don't think she stands a chance because of who *she* is."

"Oh," he said again, and it was *his* turn to make a face. "That's kind of harsh."

"I *know*," I lamented, tugging at his hand. "And I feel bad for thinking it, but I can't make myself believe anything else."

He nodded. "Otherwise . . . Halloween face."

I gave a piteous nod.

Caleb was quiet for a minute. "Why don't you try thinking about all the times your mom did something right, instead of all the times she did something wrong?"

"Because I can't think of when she's ever done something right," I said flatly.

"I can think of one huge example." He stopped and faced me. "You."

I smiled back. "You realize you just called me huge."

"I was hoping you'd overlook that," he said, pulling me forward. "What about her dress shop?"

I sucked in a breath. "Considering that's the reason we're in this mess, I wouldn't exactly call it a success."

"But she's had it for a long time, right?"

I nodded. "Since I was five." Then I grinned. "When she got the loan to buy the shop space, I asked her if she could save some of the money to buy me a tiger."

"If this story doesn't end with you getting a tiger, I'm going to be really disappointed," said Caleb.

I smiled. "I *did* get a tiger. A huge stuffed one that she bought after her first dress sale." I held my arms out wide. "Massive."

"Nice."

"Yeah, she said she was sorry for not getting it sooner but"—I paused thoughtfully—"she had to spend the loan money on bills."

"Sounds like she did the right thing," he said. "A real tiger would've been expensive to feed."

I smirked. "Yeah, but having mine was expensive too. I may have accidentally tried to ride it down the stairs."

Caleb winced. "Why do I have a feeling that didn't go well?"

I patted my right arm. "Broken in three places. Mom didn't

want to wait for an ambulance, so she wrapped me up in a blanket and ran with me all the way to Aunt Zoe and Uncle Deke's."

"Wow," he said. "She must've been seriously freaked out."

"Not really," I said. "That's one of the things I love about her. She never panics under pressure. Just starts trying to solve the problem." I chewed my lip. "Huh."

"What?"

"Maybe I *haven't* been giving her enough credit," I said. "Everything that ever goes wrong, she eventually fixes. Whether it's her fault or mine." I turned to Caleb. "And she'll fix this, won't she?"

He smiled. "I think she'll definitely try her hardest."

"I guess that's all I can ask."

He squeezed my fingers. "Do you want to go back and talk to her?"

"In a little bit," I said. "This is the first time I've been able to hang out with you in public in *normal* clothes, and I kind of like it."

We continued to walk up the road in the moonlight, listening to the crickets chirp and the mockingbirds call to one another. Occasionally, a breeze would sweep past, bringing with it the scent of wildflowers . . . and Chinese food.

I stopped. "Wait a sec."

"What's wrong?" asked Caleb.

I sniffed the air. "Do you smell that?"

He flared his nostrils. "Smells like . . . something fried."

"Out here?" We both turned slow circles, and then I saw it. Headlights just around the curve of the road.

"Are you expecting visitors on the property?" I whispered to Caleb, and pointed.

He followed my finger and immediately broke into a crouching run. I chased him, kicking up clouds of dirt in an effort to muffle my footsteps. As we rounded the curve, Caleb held up a hand to halt me, then gestured to the trees on either side. We slipped from one to the next, sidling closer to the headlights.

A car engine drowned out the words, but I could hear two people speaking, and soon I could see a lit car-top sign that read ORIENT EXPRESS.

"Someone ordered takeout?" I whispered.

Caleb shushed me and crept forward. I followed.

"Did you remember the soy sauce this time?"

I recognized the voice before the headlights even illuminated the figure.

Dylan.

My hands fumbled in my pockets until I found the game changer I was looking for. The second my conniving cousin reached for the takeout, I popped out from behind the tree and snapped his photo with my cell-phone camera. Great-Aunt Muriel would've been proud.

At the flash of light, Dylan glanced over and growled.

"Run!" I shouted to Caleb.

I was never more grateful to be back in my jeans and sneakers. Without the dress to catch around my heels, I easily outran my cousin, and as soon as I reached the light from the manor, I started shouting.

"Mom! MomMomMom! Anybody!"

"I'll get my dad," said Caleb, dashing off to the servants' quarters.

After a moment, the back door of the manor opened, along with a few windows. People poked their heads out, including Mom.

"Tori?" She looked panicked. "What's going on? What's happened?"

"Look!" I held my phone high in the air.

Mom let her head drop. "Tori, if you woke me to complain about your cell-phone coverage—"

"No! Dylan's been cheating!" I shouted.

"What? I'll be right down!" she called.

Then I realized Uncle Max was standing beside me.

Oops.

"Uh . . . I mean . . ."

He held out his hand, palm up.

"Let's see the evidence."

Without a word, I handed him the phone.

"Don't!" wheezed Dylan, trotting over. "Don't believe her, Dad."

"Son, it's hard not to." Uncle Max looked to him, eyes heavy with disappointment. "This picture is you, plain as day."

I cleared my throat. "Also, you have soy sauce on your shirt."

Dylan scowled and lunged at me just as Mom grabbed my arm and yanked me out of the way.

"If you lay a finger on my daughter, it won't be just your shoes that end up in a tree," said Mom.

"Yeah," I added.

Without taking her eyes off Dylan, Mom pushed me toward the manor. "Tori, go to your room."

"Huh? But Dylan—"

"I will handle this," she said. "Even though you think I can't."

I tugged on her sleeve. "I'm sorry I said that. I didn't mean it."

"Tori." Mom clenched her jaw. "Room."

I let go and took the tiniest step toward the back door.

"One," said Mom, counting as if I were five again.

I sighed and hurried into the manor. Angel was coming down the stairs just as I was going up.

"What's with all the yelling?" she asked.

"Dylan's about to be disqualified," I said, and kept going. I didn't hate Angel, but I definitely didn't feel as close to her as I used to.

My new room didn't have a view of the backyard, but when I sneaked into Mom's room to look out the window, it didn't matter anyway. Everyone was gone, no doubt to meet with Great-Aunt Muriel.

"She probably *should* have given the manor to her horse," I said to myself.

I could hear voices coming from the first floor, so I sprinted across the hall to my room and dove onto the bed, sending up a cloud of dust. I was still coughing when someone knocked at the door. Mom opened it and fanned the air but didn't crack one of her usual jokes.

"It looks as if Dylan is going to be disqualified," said Mom. "Apparently, tonight's takeout wasn't an isolated incident. The day we were at the airport, he called several places here and arranged for them to meet him at the property line so he could always have enough food to keep his energy up."

I sat up on the bed. "What about Uncle Max?"

She shook her head. "He says he knew nothing about it, and I believe him. The disappointment in his eyes . . . " Mom crossed to sit on the edge of my bed. "It's easy to see when you feel the same."

She might as well have punched me in the stomach and body slammed me into the floor.

"Ouch," I said. "You mean me."

Mom gave a soft laugh and shrugged. "Is there anyone else here whose opinion matters?"

I ducked my head. "I said I was sorry."

"Yeah, and you said that at the edge of the forest," said Mom, picking at the quilt on my bed. "Then later you told everyone I couldn't do it."

I didn't say anything.

"Tori, I haven't done many amazing things, but there are two that I can say I'm proud of: my dress shop and my daughter." She sniffled, and I looked up to see her eyes filling with tears. "And right now it feels like I've failed both of them."

I opened my mouth to argue, but the only sound I could produce was a squeak as my eyes welled up too. A single tear spilled over Mom's lashes and onto her cheek, and she quickly wiped it away.

"You should get to sleep," she said, sniffing again. "It's been a long night."

"Mom." I took her hand. "I thought about it, and I *do* believe in you. I swear it. You are a superwoman who does so many things. You heal me when I'm sick and cheer me up when I'm sad and put food on the table, and I've never once ever wished for a different mother, because nothing could be better than you." I paused. "Except you with a million dollars."

Mom laughed and rubbed at her eyes again. "I'd love to believe that you truly feel that way, Tori. But I can still see the worried look in your eyes." She stroked my cheek, which brought all the tears forth.

"I'm worried"—I stumbled through the tears—"because . . . I let you down! I'm . . . a . . . bad . . . daughter!" I broke down completely, and Mom pulled me to her so I could cry on her shoulder.

"Shhh," she said, rocking me from side to side. "This has been a tough experience for both of us. You're not a bad daughter. You're . . . you."

I froze and looked up at her. "That still feels like an insult."

Mom chuckled softly. "I'm grateful for who you are. It's what keeps me balanced and makes *me* notice ways I can change."

"You don't need to improve," I said. "If you were any different, we wouldn't have bathtub sundaes and graveyard hide-and-seek and Velcro Wars."

She smirked. "It *is* important for every girl to know how many stuffed animals she can stick to her body while still running an obstacle course."

There was another knock at the door, and Mom got up to answer it.

"Hello, Eli," she said.

"As you know, Dylan has been disqualified," he said. "As you *don't* know, Muriel has grown tired of this contest. Therefore, there will be one final event tomorrow morning to determine the overall winner."

"What?" I scooted to the edge of the bed. "But it hasn't been two weeks! The contest is two weeks."

He shrugged. "The contest is also hers. She can amend the rules as she pleases. Only the three families with the most points will compete. The others have been asked to leave."

Mom asked him the question that was pounding its way from my brain all the way to my chest.

"Who are the three families?"

Eli counted them off on his fingers. "Deke and Zoe Baker, Max Archibald, and Jill Porter."

"Jill Porter," I mumbled to myself, and then gave a gleeful shriek. "Mom, that's you!"

She turned to me, jaw hanging open and arms thrown wide. I jumped into them, and we hopped around the room.

"I couldn't have done it without you, baby," she said, kissing my forehead.

"Congratulations," Eli said solemnly. "And best of luck in the final challenge."

He closed the door, and Mom and I beamed at each other.

"You're going to do great," I told her, and I really meant it.

"I wonder what kind of challenge it'll be," she said. "Physical or mental or . . . " She started pacing my room, and I stopped her.

"Mom. Now isn't the time to worry. It's the time to rest."

"You're right," she said. "I should get some sleep." She smiled at me. "Thank you for our talk tonight."

I bit my lip. "So . . . are *we* okay?"

She kissed my forehead. "I could never stay mad at you. Even if you shaved off your eyebrows again and I had to make you another pair of tiny eyebrow wigs."

I wrinkled my nose. "What *did* you make them out of, exactly?"

Mom cleared her throat and stretched. "Well, I should hit the hay. Night!"

She hurried toward the door.

"Wait! What were my eyebrow wigs made of?" I pressed.

"Caleb seems like a nice boy. I hope you two had fun tonight!" She grabbed the doorknob and closed it behind her.

I stared at it and laughed to myself.

Definitely wouldn't trade my mom for anyone else in the world.

Chapter Fifteen

I'm guessing they wish I was still lost in the woods," I whispered to Mom over breakfast.

The families who hadn't made the final cut were trudging downstairs to catch the shuttle back to the airport. They were all wearing their normal street clothes and massive frowns. Directed at me.

"Well, it *is* kind of your fault they have to leave," said Mom.

"Hey!" I scowled at her.

"Sorry," she said, holding up a hand. "It's not all your fault. Your cousins should equally share the blame."

I sighed. "That's . . . better." Because, honestly, I couldn't argue with her. If the three of us hadn't frustrated Great-Aunt Muriel to her wits' end, the contest wouldn't be ending early, and the others might still stand a chance.

But now it was down to Mom, Uncle Max, and Uncle Deke and Aunt Zoe. Mom had said she couldn't see anything related to the challenge from her bedroom window, so we'd been spending the early-morning hours trying to figure out what it might be.

"Maybe it's a quiz about colonial history," I said. "Do you know any?"

Mom shrugged. "I know the big topics, like the Salem witch trials and Jamestown and the first Thanksgiving. If it's multiple choice, I should do okay."

I nodded. "Probably better than Uncle Max. But Uncle Deke and Aunt Zoe might have more combined knowledge. Let's go to the library and brush up on your history." I got up from the table and waited for her to follow.

"Great-Aunt Muriel wants maximum entertainment," said Mom. "She won't get any enjoyment out of watching four people take a quiz."

"Maybe if you guys get a finger chopped off for every wrong answer?" I asked.

Mom shook her head. "It won't be a quiz. It'll be something exciting and something where every team has an equal opportunity of winning. She might be mean, but she's fair."

"Thank you for that character reference," said a voice behind us.

Mom winced, and we both turned around to face Great-Aunt Muriel.

"Sor—" Mom began.

"Stow your apologies," said Great-Aunt Muriel. "You wouldn't have said it if you didn't mean it."

Mom blushed. "Actually, I was going to say 'Sorry you had to hear that.'"

Great-Aunt Muriel's laugh was hoarse and rusty, as if she hadn't been amused for at least two decades.

"Victoria, would you like to join myself and your cousins to view the final competition?"

I looked to Mom, who smiled and nodded.

"Go for it."

I bent and hugged her. "Win this thing quick so we can go home."

Great-Aunt Muriel watched our exchange with the emotion of someone watching a fly smash into a windshield. When I straightened and stepped away from the table, she beckoned for me to follow.

She led me around the servants' quarters to the edge of the peach trees, where four high-backed leather chairs had been positioned facing a twenty-five-foot wooden pole. Another pole had been attached horizontally to the top, like the start of a game of hangman, and from the end of that one hung a large brass bell. On the ground beneath the bell sat a huge mattress.

It wasn't too hard to guess what the final challenge would be.

As Great-Aunt Muriel and I stepped closer, I could see the tops of two heads above the seats on either end. Dylan and Angel were already waiting for the games to begin. Great-Aunt Muriel coughed, and they both peered around the side of the chairs to look at us. Angel smiled. Dylan scowled.

"Hail, hail, the gang's all here," said Great-Aunt Muriel. She took the empty seat next to Dylan, and I took the one next to Angel.

"Popcorn?" Angel offered, holding out a bowl.

"You're kidding," I said, but it smelled so good that I grabbed a handful.

"I really hope your mom wins," she said.

I stopped midcrunch. "You do?"

She nodded. "Now that I've told my parents the truth and I don't have to keep them off my back, I realize you were right. We don't need the money, and neither does Dylan's dad."

"Like heck we don't!" Dylan leaned over and frowned. "My dad promised me a new four-wheeler if we won."

"Yeah, but Tori's mom could lose her shop!" said Angel.

He shrugged. "Her mom should've handled her money better instead of being a typical chick and—" He froze when he remembered who was sitting beside him.

"Go on," said Great-Aunt Muriel, turning to face him. "I'm curious to know what the typical self-absorbed, ignorant lay-about thinks of a typical 'chick.'"

Dylan's face darkened, but he simply leaned back in his seat without a word.

"Anyway," Angel said, touching my arm, "I don't know what I was thinking. You're my friend and my family, and I should have been thinking of ways to help you instead of hurt you. Can we be friends again? I'll even share my honey hair spray with you."

I smiled. "That's *definitely* not necessary, but yes, we can be friends. I haven't been my best self here either," I said.

Angel squealed and threw her arms around me, spilling the remaining popcorn from my hand on the ground.

"Wonderful," said Great-Aunt Muriel. "Soon we'll be assaulted by geese." She reached into the folds of her shawl and pulled out a pocket watch. "Your parents should be appearing any moment now."

Dylan, Angel, and I all twisted in our seats to look behind

us. Sure enough, Mom was trudging down the hill next to Eli, with my uncles and aunt not far behind. They were all staring up at the bell connected to the beam. Aunt Zoe leaned over to whisper something to Uncle Deke.

Eli marched the parents in front of Great-Aunt Muriel's chair, and she studied them for a moment.

"Your final challenge," she finally said, "is to ring that bell. Throughout history, it has been the quickest way to announce a threat to the populace. There are, however, three rules." She nodded to Eli.

"Rule One," he said. "You cannot touch any part of the vertical support pole. Rule Two, you must complete your work where it can be seen by all, to rule out foul play. And Rule Three, the bell must be rung by hand."

"Any violation of the rules will result in instant disqualification, and the winner shall be the first person to ring the bell," said Great-Aunt Muriel. "Simple enough?"

All four parents nodded, and she clapped her hands together.

"Then let the final challenge . . . begin."

Immediately, Uncle Max broke into a run and sprinted for the barn.

"Go, Dad!" cheered Dylan.

Uncle Deke and Aunt Zoe conferred for a moment, looking from the pole to each other before darting toward the stables.

"Go, Mom and Dad!" cheered Angel.

Mom stayed at the pole the longest, as if willing it to speak the solution. Then she sprinted for the house.

"Go . . . back outside!" I said, twisting in my chair to watch as the door closed behind her.

"Disconcerting, isn't it?" asked Great-Aunt Muriel. "To wonder if she's already let you down."

"No, I'm sure she's coming up with something clever," I declared.

There was a terrible splintering, groaning sound, and all eyes went first to the pole, which remained still and calm. Then Uncle Max appeared with a long board wobbling on his shoulder.

Great-Aunt Muriel narrowed her eyes. "Is that from the side of my barn?"

Uncle Max dropped the board on the ground, and I could see the nails poking through.

"To be fair, it wasn't in the rules," I said as Uncle Max ran away again.

Great-Aunt Muriel was not amused.

Something rumbled from inside the stables, and then the

front end of a wooden cart emerged, pushed by Uncle Deke and Aunt Zoe.

"What . . . " I looked at Angel and she shrugged.

Then we both jumped as a massive white object fluttered past us and dropped onto the ground by the bell pole. A second later, Mom's head popped out of the center.

"Ha!" said Dylan. "What is she gonna do, put on a ghost costume and hope to fly?"

If Great-Aunt Muriel hadn't been between us, I would've smacked him.

It took a minute of Mom spreading out the white object for me to realize it was two bedsheets.

Great-Aunt Muriel narrowed her eyes. "Are those from one of my bedrooms?" She pointed a finger at me. "Say nothing."

I hid a smile.

Mom reached into her pocket and pulled out a needle and spool of thread. In ten seconds, she had the needle threaded and was working it in and out of the two sheets, joining the bottom of one to the top of the other. Her fingers flew along the fabric, completely undisturbed as Uncle Max threw a second board down beside the first.

"Maybe she's making a really long cape," said Dylan with a snicker.

"Maybe it's a gag to put in your huge mouth so she can think in peace!" I shot back.

"I *am* curious what she intends to do," said Great-Aunt Muriel. "Aren't you?"

"Of course," I said. "But I know it's nothing stupid like turning into a ghost or Superman. My mom's too smart for . . . OW!"

Angel was digging her fingernails into my arm. "Oh no."

I looked at her parents and jumped in my seat. "Oh *no*," I repeated.

Uncle Deke had climbed into the wagon and crouched so that Aunt Zoe could get on his shoulders.

"Did they use to be in the circus together?" I asked. "'Cuz that's the only way this'll end well."

Angel shook her head and bit her lip. "I can't watch." She covered her face with both hands. "Have they fallen yet?"

"No," I said. "I'm pretty sure you'd hear the crunch of broken bone."

Angel shifted her hands to glare at me.

"There they go!" I said as Uncle Deke slowly straightened with Aunt Zoe on his shoulders.

"Ack!" cried Angel.

"Fall! Fall! Fall!" cried Dylan.

Next to me, Great-Aunt Muriel watched with eyes alight.

Mom continued to ignore everyone around her. Every so often she'd stop sewing and tug at the seams. Uncle Max had disappeared again, but I could tell what he was doing.

I wasn't the only one.

"It shouldn't take him long to assemble that ladder," Great-Aunt Muriel mumbled to me. "Why don't you let me cut you a deal?"

Now it was my turn to block out all the sounds around us. My vision telescoped until it was just Great-Aunt Muriel and my reflection in her eyes.

"What do you mean?" I asked.

She clucked her tongue. "At the pace she's going, your mother won't win this contest, which is a pity because I was rooting for you two the most. Therefore, let me offer you a consolation prize. I will pay your bills in full so you don't have to close your dress shop."

I stared at her. "In exchange for what?"

"You simply drop out of the competition and let one of the other two teams win." She spread her hands open. "It's bound to happen anyway."

"No, thank you," I said, frowning. "I think we can still win this."

I turned away from her and tuned back in to the action.

Uncle Max was now hammering smaller pieces of wood between the two longer ones, and Aunt Zoe was straining to reach the bell with one hand while pulling out Uncle Deke's hair with the other.

"We just need a few more feet!" she told him.

Angel was peeking through her fingers. "What are they going to do now?"

Mom continued her sewing.

"Hey." Dylan leaned across Great-Aunt Muriel and poked me. "Don't forget that side bet we've got going on."

Great-Aunt Muriel raised an eyebrow. "What side bet?"

I groaned. "I have to do his homework for a month if I lose, and he has to wear a dress if *he* loses."

Great-Aunt Muriel stroked her chin. "Ah. So *that* is why you won't forfeit."

"No," I said. "I won't forfeit because I think we can win."

"I think you're about to be proved wrong," she said, pointing.

Uncle Max was propping his ladder against the beam.

"I can add five thousand dollars to my original offer," said Great-Aunt Muriel. "That's enough to pay someone else so you don't have to lift a finger helping your cousin."

"No!" I said, covering my ears.

Uncle Max put his foot on the bottom rung and tested it for security. Satisfied, he moved on to the next one.

"Tori," Great-Aunt Muriel's voice sounded close to my ear. "Why don't—"

"Shut up!" I screamed, jumping out of my chair. "I don't care how rich and important you are, just shut up!"

Great-Aunt Muriel gaped at me, wide-eyed, lower jaw shaking.

"I promised my mom that I'd believe in her." I pointed a trembling hand. "And that's what I'm going to do. You could offer me a *million* dollars, and I would still never give up on her." Tears started streaming down my face, and I turned to Mom. Panic stricken, she dropped the sheet and moved as if to come to me.

"No, don't stop!" I told her. "Keep going! You can do it!"

She froze, then clenched her jaw and nodded.

I didn't return to my seat, choosing instead to sit on the ground by her.

"How much did she offer you?" asked Mom.

"Five thousand and all bills paid," I said.

She snorted. "We're worth way more than that."

I glanced past her to Uncle Max, who was still climbing up his ladder, and to Uncle Deke and Aunt Zoe, who were now getting ready to climb on a barrel resting on the cart.

"Done!" said Mom, holding up her masterpiece . . . of two sheets sewn together.

"I'm not gonna lie," I said. "I feel slightly underwhelmed."
She winked at me. "Just watch."

Again there was a cracking and splintering sound, but this time it came from much closer. Uncle Max froze midway up the ladder and locked his knees against the side.

"Oh, boy," he said. "I knew that board looked a little flimsy."

No sooner had he gotten the words out than the board beneath his feet split in two. The sudden pressure on the board below snapped that one as well, and soon Uncle Max was tumbling onto the crash mattress.

"And now it's my turn," said Mom.

Picking up a large rock, she wrapped one end of the doubly long sheet in it and, with a loud grunt, hurled it over the top of the beam. It dropped down to the other side, taking half the sheet with it.

"Interesting," said Great-Aunt Muriel. Even Uncle Deke and Aunt Zoe stopped their mini circus act to watch.

Reaching up, Mom grabbed the bottom of both sheets and began to climb, wrapping small sections of the sheet around her foot for leverage.

"No. Way," said Dylan.

"Wow," said Angel.

"Brilliant!" I laughed, and clapped my hands.

A minute later, a bell rang loud and clear.

"We have a winner," announced Great-Aunt Muriel.

And there was much rejoicing at the future estate of Jill and Victoria Porter.

Chapter Sixteen

Dylan and Uncle Max decided not to stay after Dylan threw a megatantrum and Uncle Max finally couldn't take any more. He literally scolded his son into silence—something I never thought I'd see. "Remind me to never get on Uncle Max's bad side," I'd told Mom.

"I'm sorry y'all had to witness that," said Uncle Max. "I try to keep a civil tongue, but . . . " He chuckled. "I reckon it's time we hit the old dusty trail."

"Are you two going to be okay?" asked Aunt Zoe, taking in Dylan's sullen expression.

"Oh, sure," said Uncle Max. "We'll be doing a lot more talking, and Dylan will be getting a serious attitude adjustment once we get home. There's a corrective program that I've been meaning to enroll him in. Champs, I think it's called."

"Ironic," I said, smirking at Dylan. "Oh, and instead of one of my mom's dresses, I thought you'd prefer to remember us by wearing *this*." I held out one of my colonial dresses. "You may want to run it through the wash."

Dylan wrinkled his nose in disgust, probably at both the thought of wearing it *and* the stink coming from it.

We said our good-byes, and then Great-Aunt Muriel turned to Mom and me.

"Why don't we meet in my study with my lawyer."

Then, without waiting for a response, she hobbled up to the manor.

Mom linked her arm through mine and then led me to Aunt Zoe.

"We're going to need help managing our assets, which means a nice cut of the profits . . . if you're interested." She offered Aunt Zoe an elbow.

Angel and I exchanged excited grins.

"How can I turn down an offer like that?" asked Aunt Zoe, slipping her arm through Mom's.

The three of us climbed the lawn, like Dorothy and company off to see the Wizard, but I heard a whistling sound that made me stop. Caleb was grinning and waving from the doorway of his craft hut.

"Mom?" I asked.

She glanced back, saw Caleb, and smiled.

"We'll be inside whenever you're ready," she said.

I skipped back down the hill to join Caleb, and he hugged me and lifted me up.

"Congratulations," he said, giving me a kiss. "I made something just for the occasion."

He held out a small plaque that read PORTER ESTATES.

I hugged it to me and beamed. "You really thought we would win."

"I knew you would," he said. "Because of who you are and who your mom is."

I hugged him again. "Thank you for everything. For believing in us and helping *me* believe in us and . . . and for this." I admired the plaque.

"Just do me a favor and try to remember my family when you guys take over the property," he said with a wink. "Maybe you could keep us on as gardeners or something."

"Oh, my mom wouldn't let you go jobless or homeless, don't worry," I said. "And I actually have a good idea of how to use you guys *and* this place. I'm thinking we could lease it to the historical preservation society and make it a living colonial museum."

Caleb's eyes brightened. "That would be awesome! And I could show visitors how to do metalwork, and my mom could show them how to cook traditional . . . "

We talked for a couple of hours about how the museum could work. I didn't feel the need to join Mom inside. I trusted she'd do what was right for both of us in the end.

When it was finally time to go in for dinner, Caleb held my hand and squeezed my fingers.

"I'm going to be sad to see you go," he said, shoulders sagging.

"Me too." I squeezed his hand back. "But I'm sure we'll be coming up here a lot to check on the property and get the inheritance sorted out." I grinned. "And we'll always have e-mail."

"E-mail?" He wrinkled his forehead. "What is this strange thing of which you speak? Are you using witchcraft again?"

I laughed. "How do you think we won the contest?"

The others were already seated at the dining table—Angel and her parents, Caleb's parents, Mom, and Great-Aunt Muriel—and I took the empty space next to Mom.

"Have a good time?" she asked.

I nodded. "And I got our first proof of ownership." I showed her the Porter Estates plaque, and she smiled. I told her of my suggestion for the living museum, which she deemed "brilliant!"

"Also . . . " I said, "I was wondering if we could save some of the money for—"

"A tiger? Tori, we know how that turns out."

I laughed. "No. To keep Caleb and his family here as care-takers."

"Actually"—Mom leaned close and whispered—"they won't need any of our money. They'll have plenty of their own."

I almost fell out of my chair. "What?!"

"It turns out Muriel—"

"Has remarkable hearing," said a stout voice down the table.

Mom and I pulled away from each other and straightened in our seats.

"I was just telling my daughter of your kind nature," said Mom.

Great-Aunt Muriel gave one of her rare, rusty laughs. "Good heavens, don't lie to the child. I just happened to real-ize Charity would be dead before she had time to spend even a fraction of the inheritance. Then where would my money go?"

All other conversation came to a halt.

"So, if you're not giving it to Charity, then who gets it?" asked Angel.

We all leaned forward expectantly.

Great-Aunt Muriel crumbled croutons into her tomato soup.

Several chairs squeaked. Eli cleared his throat and coughed in a rhythm that sounded like "Mur-i-el."

Great-Aunt Muriel blew on a hot spoonful, tasted it, then made a pleased sound. She raised an empty spoon to the rest of us.

"Savory, wouldn't you agree?"

"Muriel," said Uncle Deke, turning a little pink. "Didn't you have something to tell us? About the inheritance?"

She lifted an eyebrow. "Is *that* why you're all being so quiet and polite? I assumed you'd developed manners." She lowered the spoon. "The property will go to Jill and Tori as planned, while half of the monetary assets will be given to charity . . . true charity. And the remainder will be divided equally among my family and my staff."

Cheers erupted all along the table. Everyone hugged everyone. Even Great-Aunt Muriel.

"Be honest," I said when it was my turn. "Was your horse really the reason you did this? Or could it maybe be because we're the most fascinating people you've ever met?"

"You aren't fascinating. You're mildly amusing at best," said Great-Aunt Muriel. "Henry Ford and George Patton . . . *they* were fascinating."

My smile dropped a little.

Great-Aunt Muriel took my hands in her soft, wrinkled ones. "But they weren't family," she said in a quiet voice.

I hugged her, breathing in the scent of leather and land. And then my sniffs turned to sniffles when I realized it might be the last time we'd ever meet.

"Oh, my dear," she said. "No tears, please. This is silk."

I busted out laughing and wiped at my eyes.

"Let's finish our dinner, shall we?" she asked. "My delicious soup will have gone cold by now."

We all returned to our seats, Caleb and I grinning at each other from across the table. Mom nudged me to get my attention.

"Tomorrow all the bills will be caught up," she said, "and we'll start renovations on the dress shop."

The news just kept getting better.

"You're going to take my advice?" I couldn't stop the smug grin spreading across my face.

Mom rolled her eyes. "I'm not doing it because you're right," she said. "I'm doing it because if I order more supplies, I get to see Funk *twice* a week."

"When can I start calling him Daddy?" I asked with big, innocent eyes.

But we both knew I never would. No man would ever be my

dad but the original. And Mom had taken over the role just fine.

I smirked and laid my head on her shoulder. "I love you, Mom."

She laid her head on mine. "I love you, Tori. Now please pass the artificially flavored soda."

And with that, our colonial days were over.

ACKNOWLEDGMENTS

Always for God, family, friends, and fans.

For my editor, Alyson Heller, who knows when I'm being funny and when I'm just being gross.

For my agent, Jenn Laughran, who says, "Why not?" whenever I want to try something new.

For my cover artist, Kim Smith, because, let's face it, the cover is adorable.

For my writing partners at the Lodge of Death (not as scary as it sounds . . . okay, maybe a little), who laughed hard enough for me to know I had something *and* answered questions about flying chickens.

For Jody Feldman, the ultimate game master, who indulged my dilemmas.

For Joshua Rivera, who helped me with the final challenge and lived to tell the tale.

For the Boston Public Library and its endless resources, not to mention the gorgeous interior and cozy window seats.

And for Plimoth Plantation, which made me very glad I didn't live in colonial times.

Don't miss another fun read
from Jo Whittemore!

T HERE ARE A NUMBER OF horrible ways to die at Carnegie Arts Academy. You could be crushed by a piece of falling scenery, strangled with piano wire, even kicked in the throat by an angry ballerina.

But the worst way to go would be under the daily stampede in the halls. To survive at CAA, you have to follow the crowd . . . literally.

When a swarm is on the move, it's either to reach something good (free ice cream in the caf) or to escape something bad (Jill Hudson practicing opera scales). You can usually guess the reason based on who's leading the charge, but there's always a voice in the crowd who shouts it for all to hear.

On the second Monday of January, mine was that voice.

"Play results are up!" I cried. "Know your fame or know your shame!"

The principal, who was leading a tour, pushed his group aside right before they were trampled.

"And *those* would be the ambitious students in our theater depart-ment," he said, sounding annoyed.

I wasn't sure why. We'd skipped the sparklers this year, and his new wig looked *way* nicer than the old one. It was probably less flammable, too.

Plus, we had a good reason to be excited!

Every semester, CAA's theater department put on a major perfor-mance, and every spring, it was produced by the graduating class of eighth graders. This spring, the show was an updated version of *Mary Poppins* called *Mary Pops In*. And since there weren't a lot of female parts, I was beyond nervous.

CAA followed the unwritten rule of all drama departments since the dawn of time: Any theater production should star the same three or four kids each year. Always. Unless one of them dies.

Sadly, that never happened, so I remained a bit player, tackling such gripping roles as Girl in Crowd or Villager Number Three. One semester, I didn't even make it onstage. I just shouted from behind a curtain for background noise.

My parents were *so* proud.

In my defense, it wasn't that I lacked talent. Nobody at the acad-emy had a louder voice, according to my teachers, and my best friend, Chase, assured me I was plenty dramatic. Not to mention, my mom had been a famous actress in Korean cinema. Theater was in my blood.

Yet *my* name, Sunny Kim, always fell somewhere on the bottom of the casting sheet. And when the playbill came out, I was listed under Extras, like an unpopular topping on a sundae menu.

I was the shredded coconut of the theater world.

So why was I excited about audition results this time? For starters, my friend Ilana was on the selection committee. She thought I was a good actress *and* she would keep things fair . . . unlike last year's committee.

(I burped *once* during a death scene. Like nobody has gas at a funeral.)

But this year, besides having Ilana on my side, my acting coach, Stefan, said I'd nailed my audition. It was just a matter of finding out which starring role was mine.

I sprinted toward the theater with students tussling and shoving behind me, and more joined the stampede, including Bree Hill. She and I grinned at each other, and Bree shouted something to me.

I couldn't hear her, partly because of the crowd, but mostly because of Bree's soft voice. Her shouting isn't much louder than the squeak a hamster makes when you accidentally tap-dance on it.

But Bree doesn't need volume to be a great actress. She has poise and confidence and a way of really stepping into character. I know because she and I have been audition buddies since we started at CAA. And like me, she never gets the big parts.

I leaned closer, and she shouted again.

"I'm so excited!" she said. "I'd love to be Mary Poppins . . . or even Jane Banks!" She raised her pinky and I hooked it with mine.

"I know!" I shouted back. "As long as I don't end up in the potato sack, I'll take any speaking role!"

The potato sack wasn't a theater term. It was *literally* a potato sack that had been my costume as Villager Number Three. While the main cast wore professionally tailored costumes, the ones for bit players were cheap, homemade, and badly sewn.

Bree smiled sympathetically. "You'll get something *great*. Suresh and I both think you rocked the auditions." Suresh was Bree's boyfriend and another member of the theater crowd. He always wound up with slightly better parts since he was a natural at dance numbers, but he still wasn't a Chosen One.

"Thanks," I told Bree. "Maybe lucky audition five will be the winner!"

Instead of answering she squeezed my arm and pointed at the bulletin board outside the auditorium. A sheet of yellow paper was pinned to the cork . . . a sheet that hadn't been there Friday.

Bree and I both dashed forward. The other students pressed up behind us as everyone struggled to find their names on the top of the list.

"Mary Poppins, Mary Poppins, Mary Poppins," Bree chanted over and over. Her finger settled on the name, but before I could see what was written beside it, a tall, red-headed guy stepped in my line of sight.

"Chase!" I bent from side to side, trying to see around him.

"Hey! What part did you get?" he asked.

"I don't know." I pushed him aside. "Bree! What's it say?"

Bree turned to look back at me, her expression one of sheer disappointment. "Sunny, you—"

I didn't need her to finish that sentence. The look on her face, the "S" I could clearly see her pointing at . . . I gasped and dug my nails into my cheeks.

I was Mary Poppins!

My excited shriek sounded far and wide, much to the annoyance of the kid standing beside me. With an apologetic smile, I reached for my cell phone to snap a pic of the casting sheet. Photo number one in my dust-covered album of success!

"Sunny?" Bree tapped me on the shoulder.

I shooed her away while I pulled up the camera feature on my phone. "Pay attention, people!" I bellowed to the crowd. "Something amazing has happened!"

"You've learned violence isn't the answer?" asked Chase.

I punched him and held my phone up to the bulletin board, trying to pick the best angle for my victory photo.

"Sunny . . ." Bree tugged on my arm.

"Oh! Take my picture!" I thrust the phone at her and stood against the wall, reaching up to point at Mary Poppins. "I want to . . . uh . . ."

I paused and leaned back to study the board. Now that I was closer, something seemed off. "Wait," I said, frowning. "Sunny isn't spelled S-a-r-a."

I turned to Bree, whose crushed expression had returned.

"That's what I was trying to tell you," she said, her voice quieter than usual. "Neither of us got it."

"Oh," I said. The joy that had been bubbling inside me was rapidly cooling to a sludge of shame. "Well, maybe . . ."

I searched the board for my name, hoping, praying for something almost as good. But I wasn't Jane Banks. Or Mrs. Banks. Or Mr. Banks. The sludge in my stomach thickened to a hard lump. My eyes scanned down, down, *down* the list and finally spotted my name at the bottom.

Sunny Kim . . . Villager Number Two.

I stared at the bulletin board, willing it to rearrange the letters into something else. Or to explode into a billion pieces.

Even with a friend on the selection committee, I couldn't get better than an extra. Was I really that bad?

Chase bumped against me. "All right! Villager Number Two!"

I gave him a pained expression. "I thought I was Mary!"

His forehead wrinkled. "Married? I guess you could be *Mrs.* Villager Number Two."

I stared at him. "*Mary!* As in Mary Poppins?"

"Ohhh." Chase's confused expression turned into a frown. "I'm sorry, Sunny." He put an arm around me.

"Thanks," I said. "What part did *you* get?"

Chase stiffened. "Nothing."

"What?"

"No one," he tried again, stepping away. "Definitely not the male lead."

I rolled my eyes and glanced at the casting sheet. He was Bert the Chimney Sweep, Mary Poppins's quasi-boyfriend.

Of course.

Chase *was* one of the Chosen Ones, partly because of his talent and partly because of his scruffy red hair and green eyes. He was pretty cute, and girls willingly forked over allowance to see "pretty cute."

"Awww, think of it this way." He put an arm around my shoulder. "At least you're not Villager Number *Three*!"

I took his face in my hands and smiled sweetly at him. "Hold very still. I'm going to headbutt you."

"Not his nose," murmured Bree, who was still staring at the bulletin board. "That's our moneymaker."

Chase pulled my hands away. "All I'm saying is that this role is an improvement."

"But I wanted a *lead*!" I groaned in annoyance and joined Bree. "This is so lame." I flicked the casting sheet with my fingers. "Sara doesn't even *like* being onstage. And the first time she tries out, *she* gets the spotlight?"

"Maybe she has natural talent," said Bree.

I shook my head. "Remember when she read *Macbeth* in class? I thought Shakespeare was going to dig himself up and smack her with the shovel."

"I don't think Shakespeare was buried with a shovel," said Chase.

"My point," I said, giving him a look, "is that the casting is always wrong and always unfair. I'm Villager Number Two, Bree's the . . ." I looked closer at the sheet.

"Village whisperer," she supplied.

"You see?!" I threw my hands in the air. "And we're not the only ones in ridiculous roles." I rattled off names as I scanned the rest of the audition results. "Suresh is a backup dancing chimney sweep, Anne Marie's the pigeon lady in the park, Wendy Baker's Villager Number One . . ." I paused. "How come she gets to be Number One?"

"I think because she's actually British," said Bree.

I frowned. "But she doesn't even *like* tea."

"Focus, Sunny," said Chase, eyeing the clock on the wall. "I've got five minutes before baseball practice."

CAA didn't have an athletics program, but Chase's dad wanted him to have a "sensible hobby" to balance "this acting nonsense." So Chase pitched for an intramural baseball team. He wasn't bad, either.

"Right," I said. "My point is that the starring roles in the spring production are never about talent; they're about who you know."

"Thanks," said Chase.

I grabbed his arm. "I didn't mean you. You have *plenty* of talent. Someday, they're going to rename the auditorium after you."

"That's enough," he said.

"I thought the whole point of Ilana being on the selection committee was to keep things fair," said Bree.

I snapped my fingers. "And that's why I'm talking to Ms. Elliott. She may not be running *this* production, but as the drama coach, she should know what's up, right?"

Bree and Chase exchanged a look.

"What?" I asked.

Chase put his arm back around my shoulder and steered me in the opposite direction of Ms. Elliott's office. "Sunny . . . we've been friends a long time, right?" he asked.

I nodded. "Ten years. Since you moved in down the street."

"Right." Chase smiled. "And in ten years, I've seen the look in your eyes *right now* a dozen times."

"What look?" I asked, standing a little taller. "Grim determination? Unfailing courage?"

"Insane madness," he said.

"Hey!" I ducked out from under his arm.

"It's the same look you had at seven when you tried to jump off your roof in a cape," said Chase.

I studied my reflection in a window. "There's no madness in these eyes."

"*And* last year when you asked the caf to stop serving fish so your hair wouldn't smell," he continued.

I crossed my arms. "The cute guy from my math class said I reeked like tuna."

"He was a jerk," said Chase. "You smell nice. You always have."

I blinked in surprise. "Really?"

Chase blushed. "My point is that you look like you're about to charge off and do something dumb. Don't."

Clearly, Chase didn't understand the gravity of the situation. I was meant to follow in my mom's theatrical footsteps. *Success* flowed through my veins, not the mediocrity of being The Eternal Extra.

"I *have* to take care of this," I said. "I can't go back to my parents with another bit part. And what if I'm not auditioning correctly? I need to know."

"I thought you paid that high school guy Steven to help with that," said Chase.

"*Stefan,*" I corrected him. "He changed his name when he got back from Paris."

Chase didn't look impressed. I placed a palm on his chest and pushed.

"*Go,*" I said. "If you're late, your dad's going to flip and lose the last patch of hair on his head."

Chase grabbed my hand. "Just promise you won't make things worse."

I snorted. "Yeah, it'd be tragic if I lost this part."

Chase continued to stare at me.

"I promise," I said.

I shooed him away and turned back toward Ms. Elliott's office, almost colliding with Bree.

"I'm coming with you," she said.

"I *don't* need supervision."

"Actually," she said with an apologetic smile, "I'm coming to ask Ms. Elliott about *my* part."

"Oh," I said, leading the way. "Then let's go find out why we're not famous."

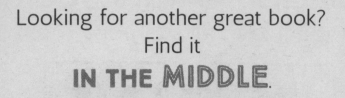

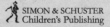

Real life. Real you.

Don't miss any of these terrific ALADDIN M!X books.

CANTERWOOD CREST
SUPER SPECIAL

CHOSEN
JESSICA BURKHART

JENNY LUNDQUIST

seeing cinderella

mix

Rules for Secret keeping

LAUREN BARNHOLDT

mix

Nice And MEAN

Jessica Leader

mix

The Hot List

Hillary Homzie

mix

Odd Girl In

Jo Whittemore

mix